Tiripsia Island

Giulia Elohi

Tiripsia Island

Volume 1
The noble of the Colombier

Giulia Elohi

© Spirit Elohi, 2024
Giulia Elohi
Pyrénées-Atlantiques
giuliaelohi.com

Cover Illustration by Odanae on odanae.com

Print on demand
Dépôt légal : janvier 2024
Loi N°49-956 du 14 juillet 1949
sur les publications destinées à la jeunesse.
Dépôt : janvier 2024

ISBN ebook : 978-2-9589073-3-4
ISBN broché : 978-2-9589073-2-7

All my gratitude to

Elizabeth, who believed in me from the beginning of this adventure. To my younger sister who accompanies me on this wonderful project. To my amazing parents.

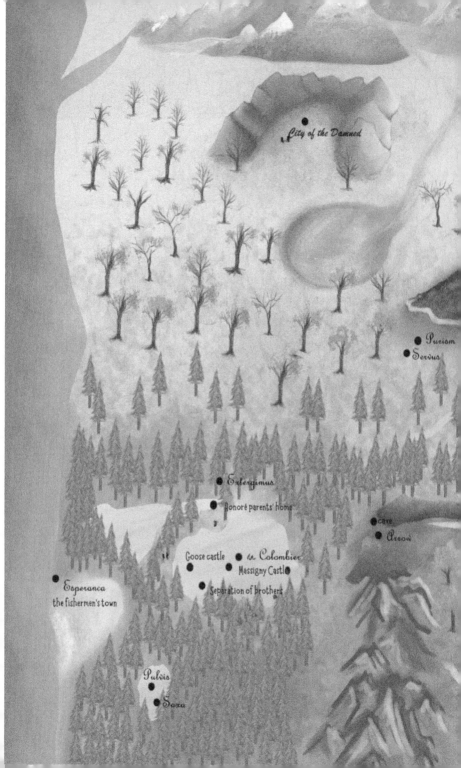

City of the Damned

Purism
Servus

Extergimus

Honoré parents' home

cave
Arrow

Goose castle   la Colombier
            Massigny Castle

Esperanca   Separation of brothers
the fishermen's town

Pulvis

Saxa

Family tree
Leusire family

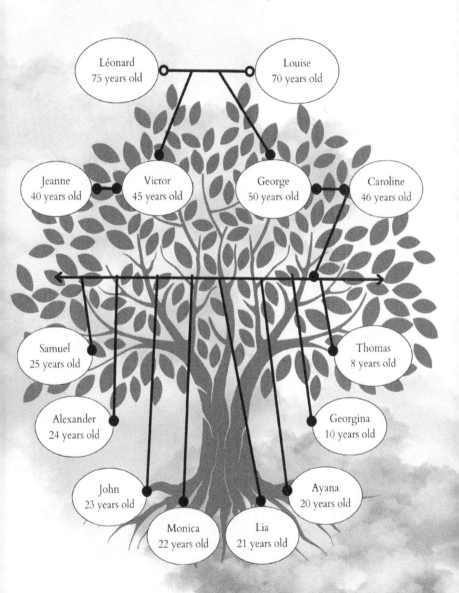

Prelude

*F*or more than a thousand years, the country had fallen back into a wild state. In the grip of desolation, the population was fighting for its survival, all of humanity had disappeared. The few good souls were being robbed and even abused. Until one day, three men from different tribes managed to join forces to reunite the people. For a time, they allowed civilization to be rebuilt, joining forces through power to create a government. For twenty-five years, they governed this island, this land, with firmness.

Their queens successively gave them children. It was around this time when the hostility began. The island was far too small for the three kings and their successors. As they grew older, each expressed a desire for more power and control. Thus, instead of being unified, this large territory was divided into three provinces.

Wars followed one long stretch of pain and blood shed after another for the throne. The sons of the kings took place of their fathers when they became too old to rule. The new kings were just as inhuman as their fathers. These young men were cruel and treacherous. Humanity plunged into complete chaos.

The wars over power continued, lasting for thirty-four years. The sons were fighting hard and fiercely for the power to control everything.

The first king, King Hilarion, held the North. He was the only one who managed to take possession of half the country. Perhaps it was on account of his cruel nature. He was an absolute monster and was known for his love of torturing people.

The south was divided into two parts. The east was ruled over by King Theodore, who was known for his greed. And the west was ruled over by King Leon. King Leon was just as bad and was considered hateful toward all women.

The kings were feared more than respected. Each king squeezed the life out of their people. Soon we will be witnesses to the greatest war of them all. The strongest of the three men will take power. The country will soon have one king and prepare for the beginning of a new day.

1

The unknown

"Eh girl, did you get lost?"

Lia, a sharp as a tack young girl turned around to see an older man with a cunning look in his eyes, standing in front of her, armed with a crossbow.

In those days, people were suspicious of everything and everyone. They lived in fear and violence. Danger was everywhere, and nobody was safe. Some people denounced their neighbors for a trifle or money, while others were only protecting their lives and those of their families. Corruption, aggression, and massacres became a frightening daily routine.

So when this man called out to her, she was wary. Although she was not shy, the ordeal she had just been through had worn her out, and made her more cautious.

"No I am not, thank you!" her braid spun as she turned around.

"It seems to me, quite the contrary. These days, it's not good to travel alone. Who knows who you might run into! Come and warm yourself by my fire." He hissed.

"Don't insist. It's no!"

His impetuosity began to annoy her. In one swift move, he seized her by the arm. She turned on her heels, drew her sword and thrust it at his throat.

"Get out of my way, I have nothing left to lose," Truth and desperation lingered across her face, his look was not just a look, it was a deep look filled with distrust with her striking cheekbones and piercing hazel eyes.

Between the trees came Spirit, her wolf-like dog with brown fur. He was enormous for a dog, which scared most people. Spirit stood next to her and growled.

The old man was not reassured.

"Calm down, calm down... A word of advice friend, what you will find further down the road is much more dangerous than me, believe me. I just want to help you. I'm lonely too. I know what it's like. Everyone needs company."

"I'm not alone," she replied in an icy voice.

"Hey kid! I didn't mean to be violent, but you leave me no choice. I'm not alone either."

And with a nod, he pointed to the groves, where men were waiting in the darkness.

"Come closer if you dare," she said, brandishing her weapon.

In attack position, her dog growled aggressively. She dodged their first arrow and grabbed the second one in her path. She threw herself at the old man, but he dodged her blows. For an old man, he was quite agile. The men jumped to surround her. She was trapped. Mastering the use of her weapons, she managed to keep them at bay.

Her dog rushed after two men in the forest. As she began to lose ground, an arrow whizzed by her ear, hitting one of her attackers. Two others fell.

The archer was a young man. He ran to stand beside her. She regained the advantage thanks to her mysterious savior. Soon, only the old man and two others were left. After one look at them, they suddenly turned and ran away like cowards.

She looked back at her benefactor, taller than her, with an imposing build, brown hair and green eyes. He had a bow and a magnificent *Flamberge*. It was the first time she had seen one. She heard about them in tales and legends. Flamberges are all wavy, with cuffs of pure gold. It is said that only legendary beings have the secret to using them. She wondered where he could have gotten it.

Her instincts told her that this man with a charming look had come from far away.

"That wasn't so bad, was it? Luckily I was around, they would have captured you, or who knows, maybe worse. They would have gladly handed you over to the walkers for mere coins."

This world had no limits. Perversity and cruelty reigned everywhere, and this was even more striking among people with little conscience and no honor. The war that was raging was generating more and more animosity.

Some people captured innocent people, raped them and then handed them over to the marchers, who worked for the kings for a few coins. They provided them with prisoners accused of treachery, theft, or suspicion of fabulation, although most were innocent. In this way, the kings using tyranny, confirmed their power and showed to all, that they were still at the top of their reign.

No one was safe. The risk was all the greater for Lia who was in the west domain under King Leon, who so despised women. She was far from her province in the east, that of King Theodore. She had to hurry to leave as soon as she had found her friends.

"Thanks for your help, but I have to go."

"Wait, where are you going? Maybe we can help each other?"

"No, I'm going alone!"

She entered the forest to look for her dog, the young man in her steps.

"Are you looking for your funny animal? By the way, I'm Emile," he said, holding out his hand.

"Listen, I have to find my dog. Maybe something happened to him."

"Sure, but I understand you're headed to Arrow. I'm headed there too. We could team up, right? Just long enough to get there, those parts are not safe for anyone."

She looked at him without saying anything, but she convinced herself that he was not going to let her go anytime soon. She gave in since he helped to save her life.

"I am Lia."

He smiled at her and they moved on quietly. Lia heard a groan and rushed forward. Spirit was lying on the ground next to some dead bodies, his paw bleeding. He was stabbed. The wound was quite deep. Emile approached, but the dog growled. Lia was worried. She couldn't imagine losing her dog that accompanied her everywhere. He meant so much to her.

"Listen up! I know a little bit about it. I have treated animals and people before. From what I see, he won't live long if I don't stop the bleeding."

She soothed her dog so that Emile could tend to him. A few moments later, he was bandaged but exhausted.

"Before arriving here, I saw a cave. We should stay there for the night. It's better not to stay in this area, believe me!"

They made a crude stretcher to carry Spirit. Night fell quickly. Shrill cries could be heard in the darkness. Emile built a fire and shared what food he had left.

"Thank you, that is generous of you."

"I would never let such a beautiful young woman starve to death!"

Lia felt like there was something special about him. She didn't know what it was or why she felt this way, but she felt as if she could trust him.

"Besides, why are you alone? And what's more, around here? One thing is for sure. You are not from here. The people who live under the reign of King Leon do not have the same taste in clothes as you."

"I'm going to Arrow to look for some friends who left there a while ago. Are you from here?"

"Oh no! I don't belong to any place. I live where the work calls me. I've had several things to do in this kingdom."

"What work are you doing?"

"I am looking for people or things. It depends."

"So you have no place or family waiting for you?"

"No, it's better this way, believe me! There are so many scary things in this world, that a family would only be a worry. Solitude works well for me. From time to time, I meet nice people like yourself!" he explained with a cute smile.

Ignoring his beautiful array of teeth, "I don't agree!" she looked away from him, "Family provides security, and they never lets you down when you need them. I'm not saying that everything is simple, but when you feel loved, life seems less complicated and sad."

"Maybe, but sometimes it's the opposite. Family drags you down. We don't all have the same luck. You're talking about your family, if I'm not mistaken?"

"Yes, I am," her glare met the floor as she realized her deep sorrow.

"Why do you look so grim? Would they let you down?" continue Emile, desperate to know more.

"Of course not!" she shot out. "It is complicated. If I am alone, it is because life took them away from me, or rather ripped them away."

"I'm sorry, I didn't know."

For a few moments, an embarrassment settled between them. Neither of them could find words to calm the discussion. Suddenly Emile's face lit up. He began to laugh, and then he told her about some adventures that had happened to him.

Although they were surrounded by darkness beyond their fire, the forest was filled with the laughter of the two new companions. Emile was a pleasant man, a little boastful but funny. He allowed Lia to forget, for a few hours, the world in which she lived.

After supper, they went to bed. Lia fell asleep, although she was plagued by nightmares that returned every night.

In the middle of the night, a shiver woke her up with a start. She heard snapping, then a growl. She got up hurriedly. All was quiet again in the blackness that enveloped her. Suddenly, a cold wind blew into the cave, which woke up her companion. Her dog had disappeared, which did not worry her particularly, since he sometimes went out in the middle of the night to hunt in the forest.

"What's going on? What is that noise?" worried Emile.

"I don't know," she answered anxiously.

They grabbed their weapons and stood their ground. The noise intensified. Closer, louder. Then, suddenly, someone struck Lia. Just before she fainted, she saw a creature striking Emile.

When she awoke, they were each locked in their own cell. Emile was a few feet away from her.

Within seconds she took stock of their situation. They were trapped in a gaping hole, their cages distant from each other, and both were placed on a rocky promontory.

"You've been inert for a while now. I don't know who brought us here, but I don't want to stay and find out. I tried everything to open the cage, but it's impossible. Even if I succeeded, there is no way to reach the mainland. I'm afraid that the fate that awaits us is not a happy one," he said, smiling silly at her.

"I saw something before I passed out. Whatever captured us, I don't think it's human. That thing ... it's weird. I've never seen anything like it. A black creature, with two long legs, sharp teeth, and small yellow eyes. Well, now that I think about it, it seems absurd. Maybe it's the shock!"

"Anything is possible. Unfortunately, I have seen things that I would rather not have seen," he said mysteriously. "Let's look for a solution. I don't want to wait to see what might happen to us."

Stuck and discouraged, they fell silent. Lia sat in the back of her cage, pensive and recalling family memories. Emile snapped her out of her reverie.

"You're thinking! What are you thinking about?"

"Have you ever been so desperate that you gave up everything, and felt like you were losing everything?"

" Sure! Who doesn't!" Emile took a deep breath. "I have had painful times that I don't like to remember. My parents abandoned me at birth. They dropped me off on a boat. Hours later, when I was a mess, people found me, cared for me and raised me. But I ran away when I was ten years old. I had just learned the truth and at that age, some things are taken with a lot of bitterness. I couldn't take it. I felt betrayed and abandoned. I lost hope and I wanted to disappear. So yes, I know how it feels. You have this black hole that never leaves you and ends up destroying you slowly. But with willpower, you can always get out of it."

"How did you do it?"

"Believe me, I am not a good example. I've been looking for a motivation to hold on to. My goal, even if it's not a glorious one, has been money. It may not be very noble, but I'm fine with it."

"Do you ever miss having a family?" Lia questioned, she couldn't imagine the latter.

"At first I thought about it, but then I told myself that the world was far too cruel for children to live in.

That it would be selfish of me to have them. There is no future here. So no!"

Silence fell again. Lia thought of her family, of the happy days, of her three older brothers who had taught her so many things, such as how to handle weapons and how to ride a horse...

"Of course! I may have an idea of how to get out of the cages. Can you pick locks?"

"Yes, but I don't have anything on me that will do."

"In my braid, I always have a pin. Here, catch it!"

It was a close call!! A minute less and the pin would have fallen deep into the cave. Luckily, Emile has good reflexes.

"Okay, but then what do we do?"

"Let's get out of the cages first!"

He jammed the pin in the lock over and over again to get it right. In the meantime, Lia had already hooked hers and climbed to the top of her cage. She assessed the distance between her and Emile's cage. His cage was closer to the ledge that would lead them to the exit.

"Be careful!" Emile was truly worried.

She took a deep breath before jumping. She managed to grab onto the wall of the cage in time. Emile grabbed her through the bars and helped her up. As he held on to her he sighed a breath of relief,

"That was close! What's next?"

"I said I would get us out of the cage. Now I need some time. Do you have any ideas?"

Emile lowered his head and began to think. He crouched down and put his hands in his jacket pockets. Suddenly his face lit up. He stood up and asked,

"Do you have anything that looks like an arrow?"

"Yes, I always carry daggers."

The creatures who had captured them had only taken their bags. Fortunately, they were not searched for weapons. She handed him the daggers and asked him,

"What's next?"

Emile smiled at her. He took out of his inside pocket a sparkling white thread. Lia's eyebrows nearly hit the roof,

"It will never support our weight!" she blurted.

"That's what you think!"

He smiled as he attached the wire to the dagger, then took a little momentum to throw it with all his might. It went into the wall opposite the cage. Emile pulled on the wire to reassure Lia of its strength. Then he tied it to a bar.

"Please, go first," said Emile amused at her but still smiling.

"Me first?"

"If it comes off, I'll be here to catch you. I won't let you down, I promise!" He placed his hand on her shoulder, hoping to give her enough reassurance to do it.

She looked at him, then realized that there was no other way. She had to try. She grabbed the wire and let herself slide. To her surprise, it did not give way under her weight. It could have even supported much more! She wrapped her feet around it and began to pull herself up towards the exit. Once she reached her destination, she waited for Emile, who had already begun his ascent. When he arrived, she asked him,

"Where does this thread come from? How can it support our weight?"

"In some places there are majestic trees with special virtues. I will show you one day. But let's not waste time. Let's get out of here!"

As they gathered their things, a roar sounded from deep within the cave. The walls shook as something came dangerously close. They began to run, dodging into the random tunnels that were available to them. They had to find an exit as soon as possible. The thing was moving very fast. Every time they thought that they were getting away, it gained more ground. Emile stopped,

"We have lost our way! We can't go on like this."

"Then we will fight!"

Determined to protect their lives, they prepared to face the creature. It slowed down in the darkness at the end of the tunnel. It was a gargantuan, shapeless creature. It moved slowly as if to savor the moment, knowing they were at its mercy, now trapped. They heard its noisy breathing coming closer, giving off a stench that took their breath away for a few seconds. As it got closer, they were finally able to see what is was by the light of the torches on the walls. It was a frightening sight. The thing was tall, black, with half-human, half-animal legs, claws on each end of its feet and hands. The latter, made up of three fingers, were a strange green color and covered with scales. Sometimes the thing crawled, sometimes it stood like a man. Its legs were stretched, similar to the legs of a frog, its chest of human appearance, but narrower at the abdomen. As for its head, it was round with pointed ears and yellow eyes. Its mouth was monstrously large, with sharp teeth and a huge tongue. And if it was possible to be worse, and stranger, it had wings, which it could fold up at will to make them disappear under its flesh.

It stared at them hungrily, emitting grunts. Intermittently, it seemed to be muttering words. And when Lia understood the meaning, it frightened her even more. It seemed to be saying "flesh", "human", "chosen", "devour". as it continued to move forward, something suddenly pulled it backward and grabbed it by the neck.

It was Spirit who had just saved them. Without missing a beat, Emile shot an arrow into the creature's eye, and it let out a heartbreaking scream. Lia cowered with her hands over her ears. Emile took her by the shoulder and urged her forward.

They followed Spirit to the exit, but kept running. Loud screams echoed behind them.

Suddenly, Lia was grabbed by the calf and dragged back to the cave. Emile came to her rescue. He managed to kill whatever had grabbed her. When she got up, she saw a horde of satyrs charging at them.

She was able to recognize them thanks to the stories that Nanou, her nanny, had told her at night when she was little. Even, that wasn't allowed.

They were small men with goat's feet instead of legs. Emile and Lia took up an attack position. They threw arrows at them, then took out their swords. There were many of them, but they were not armed. The two friends were ready to fight, when all of a sudden, with fear in their eyes, the satyrs retreated.

Lia and Emile took advantage of this moment to escape. They didn't know how long they had been running, but it seemed like an eternity. When they were far enough away, Emile built a fire. It was already dark.

"We spent more than a day in that cage. Do you think we are far from Arrow?" said Lia tormented.

"I would say a little less than a day's walk."

Lia reclined, worried about the fate of her friends.

2

Arrow

*A*fter a few hours of walking, the end of the day was approaching. The leaves were shaking in the sudden breeze as Lia's mind raced with thoughts of her friends. She was startled. Even though Lia was small in stature and very athletic, each of her steps seemed heavier than the last. The forest became darker as night replaced day.

Neither Emile nor Lia spoke. It was as if they both knew that silence was a way to listen out for any suspicious noises. If they were attacked, they might have a chance to hear them coming. Only the footsteps of Spirit's comings and goings disturbed their peace.

Emile kept glancing behind him, when suddenly he stopped dead in his tracks. Lia eyebrows swiftly pulled closer together. Her thin lips were shut tight, as her jaw became tense as she wondered, *" … facing these creatures again is not a good idea. My time is running out… I have to find my friends."*

"Run!" shouted Emile.

They ran as fast as their legs could carry them. Several footsteps behind them could be heard, and from a distance they could see the edge of the woods. They were not safe in this forest, but even less so in the open on the plain. Moving in this direction was not a good idea, but Lia trusted Emile. No sooner had they reached the road than they hit a hard mass that knocked them to the ground.

"Easy friend, you are scaring my horse. Well, you look like you just saw a ghost!" said a man staring at them strangely.

"You could say that," said Emile, helping Lia to her feet.

"Be careful next time," the man replied in an unfriendly tone.

Emile was not impressed and asked.

"Where are we? How far away is Arrow?"

"Oh no buddy, see that hill? Arrow is right behind it!"

Emile turned to Lia.

"I don't know what was behind us, but hopefully it won't go any further."

She slowly nodded as she remembered this fact.

Now she had to find her friends as soon as possible and leave these borders. She didn't want to stay here another minute.

She asked Spirit to wait for her here. She was certainly not comfortable leaving him, but Arrow was a city of hunters. He was safer alone. His instincts would help him to flee in case of danger. At least, that's what she hoped.

"What attacked us in the cave? Were they satyrs?"

"Yes, they are stubborn by nature."

"Have you met any before?"

Emile's eyes narrowed, remembering his encounters. "Sometimes during some of my quests. They are vile and violent beings."

"But in the fables they are good..." her angelic face seemed to match her child-like response.

"In the stories perhaps! There has never been any humanity in them. They serve evil, that's all you need to know. If you come across them again, don't think and kill them. Let's keep moving!"

Until now, Lia had not had the opportunity to reflect on what had happened to her. These things she had come across were not supposed to exist. She had been told stories to scare her. It was a way to get the unruly ones to obey. She never thought it could be true. Although she wanted to know more, her priority for now was to reach her goal. Only the present moment was important. That's what her father would have told her.

Arrow was finally in front of her!

People came from far and wide to shop there. The dense forest that surrounded the city was populated by the largest species of animals ever recorded. Although Lia thought this was wonderful, the people saw it as nothing but wealth.

The city bordered the crossing of the other two kingdoms. Surrounded by cliffs, it had only one entrance, which was the only way to enter the domain of King Leon. The entrance was well guarded and no one could enter without being seen.

Once in the domain of King Leon, it was necessary to walk a few kilometers through the forest to reach a hill, and finally discover the village of Arrow located below.

The city was not wide but very long. All the houses were stuck to the walls of the rocks. The town had no gardens or greenery. The only vegetation was the surrounding forest. All the houses looked the same. They were made of wood and had no floors.

In fact, everything in this city was made of wood. Gravel dotted the alleys, and the rest was just dirt. Many decorations adorned the town and hundreds of statues of hunters who had killed animals in the forest. As for the others, they represented animals that could be hunted with impunity.

Two constructions stood out from the others. One was a bell tower and the other a stone house which stood opposite each other in the middle of the city. The bell tower was covered with mysterious symbols.

Lia had already heard about it from her brothers when they came here. Arrow was the only city in the kingdom that welcomed foreigners to do business there. But no one was allowed to go any further into the country, although no one really wanted to anyway.

When you belonged to a kingdom, it was impossible to change it. If by chance you managed to hide out within a different kingdom, you would be sentenced to death.

A villager interrupted them.

"Hello friend! I'm in charge of controlling who comes in and out of our town. First, I need a name and a profession!" his tone sounded deceptively friendly.

"I'm Arthur, I'm a shopkeeper, and this is my wife who accompanies me. Her name is Elizabeth," Emile winked at Lia.

She looked at him sideways, but refrained from commenting, thinking it was the right thing to do.

"A few tips before we let you pass. The building you see in the middle is the bell tower, the hunters' landmark. It tells of our past wealth and our present prosperity. The house in front of it is our governor's house. As a buyer, you can examine our statues, which are all kinds of animals of different sizes found in our forests. This is our pride and joy, and I tell you, we are the best in the WHOLE country. Have a nice trip in our country," he said hastily, turning quickly to another stranger.

Lia greeted him and walked into the village. As she took a quick look around, she became confused at the sight of thousands of people. She had of course, heard about the notoriety of this town that attracted people, but the chance to find her friends was getting slimmer.

She passed by the statues, each one as crude as the next. The hunters with their prey, posed like kings. Lia felt uneasy. Emile beckoned her forward. The people who lived in Arrow were all dressed in green. Far from being friendly, most of them walked around with pride and a haughty look in their eyes, shoving strangers in their path. Outraged by such behavior, Lia turned to Emile.

"Have you been here before? This place is strange and so unwelcoming."

"It exudes absurdity and pride. King Leon himself being very proud, allowed this village to admit anyone who wanted to do business, hence the ease of access. Beyond that, you don't go unnoticed. If you go further up past this village, the people look like the people around here. But each village has a recognition mark so that everyone can be identified. So I advise you never to go beyond the borders of this village if you can."

"If there's nothing to worry about, why the fake names?" Lia was puzzled and had to ask.

"Caution is still required. When you leave, say that I sent you home, it will look less suspicious."

Lia nodded, it was time for her to go and look for her friends, but the crowd of people in this city worried her.

"I think it's time to say goodbye. We both have things to do. Thank you for everything. I have to find my friends and go back to the forest to look for my dog. I don't like the thought of him being alone with those hunters lurking around."

"One thing ... again! When you leave, say that your friends are slaves," he took a paper from his pocket. "Here is a man who owes me a favor. He will give you a false declaration of sale," he looked at her for a moment, giving her chills. "It's a farewell then! Our roads will now separate. I am happy to have met you. I hope that one day our paths will cross again."

Emile made a pretty curtsy and took her hand to kiss it.

Without knowing why her heart tightened, Lia glared at her ankle boot before answering.

"Who knows!" she said quickly. "If you believe in destiny, one day maybe..." feeling a warm sensation from her cheeks.

As Emile parted ways with her, his hand brushed against hers. He winked over his shoulder and shouted,

"I hope so. I've never known such charming company."

He turned around but Lia followed him with her eyes for the last time, losing sight of him through the crowd.

She came to her senses and looked for a friendly face. She had to find some clues to know where to start looking. A little further on, a man was leaning against a wall and bowing to some ladies.

He was a salesman of clothes and bric-a-brac. As she stepped forward, the man smiled at her.

"Well, pretty lady, you have come to the right house. Your eyes would be magnified with a hat. Ah, ah!" He paused, "well, looking at it, your air tells me that it is not what you are looking for. Perhaps, a coat or gloves to suit your beautiful golden skin?"

She interrupted him.

"Excuse me. I'm not looking for any of that. It's information that I need. I am lost and my friends must be worried. Were there any strangers around here looking for refuge?

The man's eyes raced from corner to corner.

'Yes, but if I were you, I wouldn't talk so loudly. Novelties like that are frowned upon here. If you're looking for them, they're probably in the bell tower. There are prisoners there. They are being interrogated before the execution.'

'The,' Lia cleared her throat, 'the execution? I don't understand?'

'Apparently they are deserters. Listen, I'm doing you a favor. Run, leave. If you've come to look for someone, say goodbye and go away. Because you won't find help here.'

She continued on her way to the bell tower. She had to find a way to get in. However, it was well guarded. From a distance, it didn't look so huge. On the plus side, the access was rather easy for Lia. The walls had hooks and hatches, which would allow her to climb up easily. Naturally skilled at climbing anywhere, it will be child's play for her. Even so, she would have to climb without attracting attention.

She quickly lost hope. There was no way that she could scale the building without being noticed. It was too well guarded. She decided to wait until nightfall, hoping to sneak in without being seen. She went to a shop and waited.

She came out of her thoughts when someone sat down at her table.

It was Emile smiling.

'What's a pretty girl doing sitting alone at a table? Aren't your friends with you?'

'There were some complications.'

'I came back because I heard the story of the deserters and the sentence. I thought you were probably going to do something foolish. Am I right?'

'I have no choice!' she nearly growled, clenching her fists.

'It's doomed to failure!' he nearly shouted, then quieted down.

She looked at him, disconcerted. Emile smiled back at her before continuing.

'I bet you're going to try to break into these walls and for that, you need a man with skills and ideas. So me!' he boasted. 'Having done business here in the past, I know the place well. The only way for you to do this safely is to go to the east side of the building. It is the most accessible and least visible. At nightfall, people gather on the west side to celebrate the full moon, which is said to encourage the gathering of animals. You must have been born under a lucky star, because tonight is the full moon! After the sun sets, there will be a change of guards. I'll distract them while you get into the bell tower, then you're on your own. Right now, there are only two guards inside, but there will be more in the morning. After picking up your friends, find the door leading to the underground tunnel. It leads directly to the governor's house. I'll wait for you there. Afterward, I'll let my imagination run wild.'

" You forgot one detail. How will you get into the governor's house?"

"I already have an audience with this dear governor. Some people owe me favors, people in high places." He glanced at her, admiring her athletic yet lady-like build, "Anyway, let us not delay. Let's get ready. It's getting dark. Above all, once inside the governor's house, say that you got lost and that you are with me. One last detail, bring only your friends with you. If there are more of you, I won't know how to explain it."

She nodded in response and they left the tavern.

When they arrived on the east side, Emile signaled her to wait. The mission was supposed to be simple, but Lia doubted her skills more than ever. If Emile did not manage to keep the guards away, all would be lost.

As he approached, he simulated a state of drunkenness. He staggered perfectly. One of the men gave him a blow on the backside, which made him lose his balance. But he played his role perfectly. He fell down gently and continued his performance. Two other men came to watch the show. It was the moment! Emile had the attention of all the guards who had moved away from their posts to have some fun with him.

It took Lia a moment to get to the top. As she approached, she heard voices inside. She leaned a bit closer to their window to discover two men in black discussing the fate of the prisoners. She leaned in even closer and saw her friends huddled among the other prisoners. Looking a little higher, she saw a narrow but accessible entrance for her height. She was the smallest of her family. She managed to pull herself up to the opening, but it was not easy.

Once inside, she analyzed every angle. She jumped from beam to beam to reach the center of the room. From there, she had an adequate overview of the place to develop her plan. She had to act now.

She jumped one last time on a beam that was just above the guards. Once there, she jumped on the first man. This was followed by blows and dodges. One of the men managed to throw her to the ground. The other threw himself on her to subdue her. She succeeded in giving him a headbutt. He went crashing to the ground.

While she was still being held by the guard, one of her friends, Kéo came to her rescue. He grabbed the guard and threw him to the ground. The second guard, still on the ground, picked up candlestick and hit Kéo in the head. Kéo collapsed. Using a nearby bench, Lia jumped behind her first attacker and hit him in the head. There remained only the guard with the candle. She dodged it with difficulty.

Suddenly he fainted. Rose, another friend of Lia, had picked up another candlestick and hit him. Then she rushed to Kéo, who was coming to his senses.

The people in the room were frightened and stood still. Lia tied up the guards, then joined her friends and hugged them.

"Kéo, Rose, are you okay?"

"Yes, we're safe, but we have to leave right away," Rose hurried.

"I have a plan. A friend of mine is having a meeting with the governor. When we find the underground passage to his mansion, he'll help us get out of there."

"Wait, what about the others!" interrupted Kéo.

"I can't do anything. I am sorry!"

She watched them for a few moments, and then gave in, taking the key from one of the guards and throwing it to them. No one moved. Some looked away.

"Well, now let's go. They have a way to escape. It's up to them to take matters into their own hands."

Not knowing which way to go, Lia tried the first door, while Rose and Kéo took the others. Opening the door on the west side, Rose came across a staircase that went into the darkness. She called out to her friends. They descended the stairs one by one, torches in hand. The spiral staircase seemed endless. It was like a descent into the depths of the earth. The air was getting more and more stuffy, and it was getting darker and darker. With relief, they finally reached the basement. Lia raised the torch and discovered a bottomless corridor.

"Finally, we are here," says Kéo. "However, I will feel better in the open air!"

"Let's get out of here as soon as possible," Lia replied.

After a few steps in the long corridor, they opened a door to what appeared to be the governor's house. Not much could be seen. There seemed to be no windows at all.

Lia touched something hard but slimy. Kéo held up the torch. It was just a piece of meat.

They had landed in the pantry. The room was huge and the amount of food in it was disproportionate for one man. He was said to be petty and a big eater, so it must be true.

Once out of there, they found themselves in a hallway. Lia hoped that Emile had arrived by now. Otherwise they would not be able to justify their presence.

"Hey, who's there?" a guard called out to them.

"We are travelers who have come to bargain," Lia replied.

"So what are you doing here? Do you have a permit?" the guard aggressively asked.

"We got lost admiring the your beautiful buildings. We were with Arthur," she kept her tone soft and steady.

"Ah! Arthur, of course. Are you his wife?" his tone perked up at the sound of Arthur's name.

"Yes," lied Lia, internally sighing.

"He's an amazing man, he comes here often, and this is the first time he's talked about you. He is secretive, isn't he?"

"Yes, yes. Can you take us to him?" pretending to be impatient.

"Wouldn't you rather wait here?"

"I won't ask twice!" Lia continued to play her role.

"Well, follow me," whispering he continued, "I would have warned you!"

She did not immediately understand the meaning of his last remark and walked with a heavy heart toward the floor. She had a bad feeling and wanted more than anything to leave this place.

Upstairs, they passed a brothel where many women were having a great time seducing men who were probably married and rich.

Lia found Emile surrounded by young women courting him at will. When he saw her, he felt uncomfortable.

"Dearest, here you are at last. I'm doing some research for our next merchants."

"Well, let's get out of here, shall we?" Lia pretended to be humiliated and vexed to find her man in such a posture. She noticed that she hardly forced her game.

"Well, ladies, if you'll excuse me. It was a pleasure," said Emile, taking a bow.

They were heading for the exit when a man appeared before them. He was stout, with a chubby face, small blue eyes, a large nose, a sickly look, and greasy brown mid-length hair. He walked forward with disgrace as if he owned the world and looked at Lia greedily, undressing her with his eyes.

"Well, well, my dear friend, you didn't say goodbye to me? Aren't you going to introduce me to your beautiful lady?"

"Excuse me for this rudeness," bowing to the man. "This is my wife Elizabeth and our two companions. They help us carry our goods. My dear, this is the governor duly called *The Chosen One*."

"Delighted, my dear," he said while leaning in to kiss her hand. "You should come more often. I rarely see such beautiful and mysterious young women. Arthur, you had hidden this treasure from me. Why don't you and your wife come to my house for dinner tonight?" his tone was strong and almost sounded like a demand rather than a question.

"I..." Lia began.

"We'd love to. Thanks again for the meeting, Governor," Emile cut in.

The governor took Lia's hand and kissed it greedily, which repulsed her.

"See you tonight, *my dear*."

They left the house, exhausted but relieved.

"It's time to get out of here. Let's get out of this damn place," said Emile.

"Totally agree," said Kéo, holding out his hand. "Thank you for helping Lia get us out of here. Why does the governor call himself *The Chosen one*?"

Emile cleared his throat before answering, "He says that he saved the world, that he is the only one who started from nothing, considering himself to be the best. He gave up his real name and chose this one, which according to him characterizes him very well. He is a vile man. It is better that Lia never crosses his path again, especially alone. He loves only two things in life, food and women. In fact, he considers women as meat and sometimes mistreats them. He has his eye on you Lia, and this is a bad sign. When he wants something, he usually gets it, no matter how. They say that he pays the debts of some men to sleep with their wives, who have little choice. The sooner we get out of here, the sooner we'll be safe. I can say goodbye to this city for good because *The Chosen One* will be very angry that we didn't show up at his dinner."

"I'm sorry," Lia replied. "You came here looking for something and because of me you didn't even have time to finish your quest."

"Oh, I wouldn't worry about that if I were you," he said strangely.

They began to walk briskly toward the exit.

Suddenly an echo resounded throughout the city. A guard had just sounded the foghorn from the bell tower. Emile's eyes widened. He held his breath and turned to Lia, Kéo, and Rose.

"This is a very, very bad sign. I never heard it ring before. Someone must have noticed that some of the convicts have run away. Unfortunately for us the governor is calling in the executioners. And believe me, having them after us means death. I'm sorry Lia, but only you and I have a chance to leave and stay safe. With what's going on, they won't let any supposed slaves leave Arrow without making sure they're who they say they are," then, turning to Kéo and Rose he spoke gently. "I'm sorry for you. There are some circumstances that you can't fight, even with the best will in the world."

"That's because you don't even try! I won't give them up. Go! I understand. For you, we are only strangers. Thanks to you and good luck!" answered Lia bitterly.

Then she turned around. Emile looked at them for a moment and left, leaving them with no solution.

"Lia, maybe you should listen to him. Kéo and I will figure it out."

"No, I have come this far to find you. Only you remain. I will not abandon you!"

Suddenly, a hand grabbed Lia's arm. She turned around. It was only Emile.

"We arrived together and we will continue together. I refuse to leave you. But we'll have to be smart to get out of here."

"Who are these men who are after us?" asked Lia.

"Executioners, trained in cruelty, but no time to talk. Let's go!"

They arrived at a tavern, went inside and took a table in the back, away from prying eyes and ears.

In a low voice, he explained his plan.

"I see only one way, and I hope it works. It is to cause a riot. Have people hear you say that people have escaped, and if they don't find them soon, they'll pick up strangers in their place because they have to bring in guilty people at all costs. Then you will leave, saying that you don't want to stay another minute risking your life here. I'll try to spread the rumor around. When it's over, we'll be waiting at the third house on the east side. Good luck!"

When Emile left, they remained pensive and silent for a few seconds. They were facing a complex situation with little chance of survival.

They got up and sat down at the most prominent table of all. Kéo asked Rose to get them drinks, then turned to Lia.

"I want you to make me a promise. If we ever find ourselves in an impossible situation, promise me that you will save your life and Rose's."

"We won't have to make that choice. We'll be fine."

"Really? Let's face it since what happened at the Colombier, there's not much hope left. So I want you to make me this promise!"

"Of course, I make that promise to you. But if you give up hope now, what will be left for her? I've never seen you give up, so why now? You taught me never to give up. Even in the most desperate situations. That even through the darkest of circumstances, there is always a spark that we must keep alive!"

"Are you okay here?" said Rose, who was coming back with their glasses.

"All right, let's get started. We've wasted enough time!"

Lia looked at Kéo with determination, then began her speech. It didn't work. She tried a little harder, but no reaction.

Then a young boy picked up his ball that had slipped to their table. As he walked away, he told his mother, who listened to them. Then came the worried looks that grew more and more frightened.

When they left the tavern, they were no longer alone. Lia regained hope and wondered if Emile had succeeded on his side. There had to be a lot of them, otherwise, it would have no effect.

They walked hurriedly toward the third house, their hearts clenched. She hoped with all her heart that it would work. As they approached, they saw Emile leaning against the wall of the house.

"It worked! In the city, people get nervous and, panic. Let's wait a little longer and then we can leave. Above all, let's stay together. When we go through those doors, we have to stay together and run as fast as we can without stopping to get as far away from here as possible. It's going to be very fast. We won't have much time before the backup arrives."

At that very second, a hoot went up. The crowd was moving forward, worried and panicked. The few guards who were there tried to contain the crowd. The watchman tried to reason with them.

"Calm down! What's going on? You know that we don't allow you to get out of here that easily. It will take time, so be patient!"

This speech gave the crowd a sense of madness. The crowd moved on one accord. Then, under pressure and in a hurry, the first men began to rush and hit the guards to escape.

Emile signaled for them to run. Kéo and Rose followed him hand in hand. They went through the door and began to climb the hill.

Once at the top, Lia turned around and saw men on horseback, wearing long, black, hooded pilgrimages that covered them from head to toe. They drew their blades to stop the men who tried to run away by slitting their throats with their swords.

One of the men in black ordered the others to catch up with all fugitives. Lia joined her friends, feeling saddened and guilty about the deaths. But they had to run.

They entered the forest. The beast that usually roamed these woods frightened Lia, but she had no choice but to take this path.

After a few minutes of running, they slowed down, exhausted.

"Don't stop. It's still too dangerous," shouted Emile.

Suddenly Spirit came out of nowhere, and ran towards Lia, who embraced him. Then she got up to continue running.

Suddenly a whinnying sound came from behind them.

A man on horseback galloped towards them at full speed, sword brandished. Spirit jumped on the horse, tipping it over. The man rolled and landed on the ground in front of them. Emile drew his sword to face him. Spirit jumped on him, but the man was gifted with impressive strength and pushed him back with ease. Lia also drew her sword.

Kéo and Lia attacked. Exhausted, Kéo lost ground and was thrown further away from the battle. Lia advised Rose to move away with Kéo. Emile got up and with one blow of his sword he split the robe sleeve cloak he was wearing in two. The latter touched the ground and caused the fugitives to become stricken with fear. The man, as if scalped, had no skin left on him, only flesh and deep marks of torture. His mouth was wired shut.

This moment of curiosity allowed the enemy to retaliate and strike Emile in the arm. Emile dropped his sword. The man focused on him, forgetting Lia's presence. She drew her bow and pierced his neck. He screamed before drawing his last breath.

"What was that thing?" asked Lia as she ran to Emile.

"The foghorn awakens them and warns anyone who wants to defy the law. They only kill on the orders of the governor."

"Are they humans?" continued Kéo.

"At one point in time, yes. But through years of torture, they have become beasts … monsters. But I don't know where they get their strength from. Let's go. There may be others after us!"

"No!" Rose said firmly. "Let me at least cover your wound."

"We'll do it later!"

"If I were you, young man, I would listen to my wife.

Rose looked at him unyielding, and Emile gave in.

***

After three days of walking, they finally arrived at their territory, the domain of King Theodore. The long journey had exhausted them.

After moving further into their land, they found a spot in the woods to rest. While Rose checked on the healing of Emile's arm, Lia broke the silence.

"Thank you Emile. You saved our lives."

"Yes, thank you," replied Rose. "To the both of you. Lia, you did not abandon us. We are grateful to you. But I must ask you a question, what happened to our village? By now, there must be nothing left but ruins and ashes. The number of people I saw die… But what happened?"

The Colombier

*T*hree months earlier, Lia and her family were at their estate called "Le Colombier," in a manor house of the same name, located in the village of "The Molière" in the southwestern part of the province of King Theodore.

The Leusire family has lived there for two generations. Her father, George Leusire, ran the estate with a firm hand. As for her mother, Caroline, she supported him with determination and sensitivity. They had met while her mother was traveling in this region, and she had acquired her title of nobility by marrying him.

Very few knew then the importance and luxury of having land and personal wealth. George inherited this wealth from his father, and therefore ruled as governor.

Together they had eight children. The eldest, Samuel, had all the features of his father, robust with brown hair. He had his father's fighting spirit and was raised from an early age to govern and take over the family business, which Samuel learned with talent. Next in line was, Alexander, the family's don Juan, who spent his time climbing the walls of villages and houses. He was an excellent climber, just like Lia. John, their third child, knew how to handle weapons, but always behaved with wisdom. Then came their daughters Monica, twenty-two and Ayana, twenty who was a year younger than Lia. Monica who follows directions flawlessly. She carried out the values of protocol with conviction. Ayana, with her cheerful character, liked to follow Lia in her crazy adventures. Then came the younger children, Georgina, ten years old, calm and patient by nature. Then, Thomas, eight years old, who already liked to spy and make everyone he met go crazy. He couldn't stand orders, which made him very insolent.

As nightfall approached, Lia knew she should have been home a while ago. She had settled down at a table in the tavern in a village, not far from *the Colombier*.

When she got up to leave, a group of men burst into the tavern and not the least, they were all from the North. She could tell by their rags. Like her, all the inhabitants of the tavern paid particular attention to these people, wondering what they were doing in their country. This was not a good omen, but rather a sign that war would soon be knocking on their doors, and that her brothers would soon be enlisted on a battlefield. She did not want that.

The three men sat down and ordered beers. One of them caught her eye. He was normal for a northerner, tall, and strong, but his hair was a gray she had never seen before, and his face was covered with symbols, which made him unusual, even strange. Suddenly he stood up, sweeping the room with his eyes before speaking.

"Men and women of the Molière, we come first as friends. And it is as a friend that I will make you this proposal. Follow us, and fight for King Hilarion. We are on the eve of the greatest war ever known. If you have heard certain legends, certain rumors about our king and what he has found, I can confirm that they are true. Yes, he has allied himself with the strongest, especially the wizards. A friendly piece of advice, from tonight pack your things, and join us at sunrise. To those who decide to stay, know that we will return with an army. We will pillage, kill, and rape so that nothing remains on the lands of Molière. It's up to you, make your choice. See you tomorrow in front of this inn. Good evening to all!"

He left with a petty smile. Like everyone else here, Lia remained petrified. After two deep breaths, she left her table with a decided step. She wanted to warn her family, but she preferred to go first to her friends, those on the other side of the village, far beyond the river. She had to warn them of the danger, even if it meant taking a longer detour.

When she reached the path, she heard footsteps coming closer and closer. Not knowing what it was, she decided to hide behind a bush. The events that had taken place at the tavern made her cautious. Through the woods, an animal appeared. It was of an imposing size, beige and long-haired. It took Lia a moment to recognize it as her dog Spirit since the night was unusually dark. If Spirit was out and about, then that meant that her family must be looking for her. Lia emerged from the bush and Spirit ran to meet her. As she cuddled him, a figure appeared in the short distance. It was her brother Samuel.

"Hey sis!! We've been looking for you for an hour! Where have you been? Don't say anything ... you were at the tavern, right?"

"Yes, but there was..." she answered, getting up hastily, ready to defend herself before her brother interrupted again.

"Don't worry, we know everything. You weren't quick," he smiled at her, "Master Eliad beat you to it. He was on horseback when the people of the village came out of the tavern in a panic. Let's go back. I have work to do."

Eliad the master of arm, was sent after her like always, when she makes her dad angry. He actly moslty with her like a father. Close age like his dad, forty-five years old, vigorous, with brown hair and gray eyes.

"No, I have to go see Kéo and Rose. I have to warn them."

"NO, you go home. That's an order!"

"It seems to me that I don't have to take orders from you," she stopped talking before saying something to Samuel that she didn't mean. Taking a deep breath, she continued, . "Listen, I'll be back soon. I won't be long. I just need to warn them." She tried looking deeply into his eyes to catch a faint glimmer of sympathy.

"No, Father is waiting for you. I don't think you want to make him any angrier than he already is?"

She took her air of seriousness and kept her comments to herself. She knew that he was right.

In the past, she had come back later than she was allowed to and suffered strong consequences. But she never came home at an unreasonable hour, and today was not the day to try. It could wait until tomorrow.

As she walked forward, Samuel embraced her, then preceded with her on the way back.

When they arrived at the house, her brother pushed her to go inside. Fear riddled across her face. She was apprehensive about her father's reaction.

With the arrival of the Northmen, he might already be furious.

When Lia gathered herself together, she found her father in his office with his two brothers. He stared at her with a serious and angry expression, then motioned for her to sit on the couch.

George's office was the largest room in the house. It was meant to hold and welcome many important people. Her father needed to manage accommodating large groups of people at any time of the day, both at lunch and dinner; this explained the oversized table built in the middle of the room.

He brought out the valet, who was in charge of this place.

"I usually get angry when you go out of bounds in this house, but now you come home at unacceptable hours when a lady has no business being out. What upsets me is that I see that I have been far too lenient with you. This evening showed me that it is too dangerous to let you venture out at such an hour. From now on, my daughter, know that you will not leave this house after lunch hour. You will be confined to your room. Outside this house, Eliad will follow you in your every move. I am grateful that Eliad warned us of this evenings threat," then, turning back to his brothers who were at the end of the room. "Alexander go and look for Nanou to tell her that I am finished with Lia and that she should take her back to her room."

Before her brother John came out, he smiled at her as he did every time she was punished, to encourage her.

This time she was just as angry as her father. She didn't understand why she had to be punished like this. The men from the North had entered their kingdom and it wasn't her fault.

"But Father, it is unfair to deprive me of my freedom. You know how important it is for me to meet the people of our own village. They trust me, and you can't forbid me to go as I please."

"My daughter, what I just told you is not debatable at all. The punishment is already quite flexible. If you answer me one more time, I warn you that my decision could be even more sectarian!"

She wanted to speak up again to defend herself. When it came to protecting a cause that was dear to her, and although her father was a fierce and impressive man, she knew how to stand up to him.

John understood her intentions and grabbed her by the shoulder, cutting her off before she could say a word.

"Father, let me take her back to her room myself. I'll make sure she doesn't disobey. Emotions have been running high tonight. Let's limit the drama."

"So be it! But come back as soon as possible. Urgent business requires the meeting of the men of the family."

With these last words, her father looked deeply at her one last time and turned his back on her. Lia violently opened the door and went towards the stairs with tears in her eyes.

John ran to her.

"Don't worry. He'll calm down. You would be less stubborn if you knew what was at stake."

She stared at him reproachfully. Just as she wanted to answer him, he anticipated her.

"I know there are things that hold you back beyond our walls. But know that sometimes it is wise to let go, even though it is difficult and unethical. But that's what growing up is all about. Sis," he stopped in front of Lia and took her by the shoulders, "I want you to listen to me carefully, and for a few days at least, do as father says. It is imperative that you obey him. If you don't do it for father, do it for me and for your family, your sisters... I promise you that in a little while you will be able to do what you like again. Promise!"

"Okay! But what about Rose and Kéo? They have a right to know what's going on. They will be the last to know, or worse, it will be too late. As you know, they never go to the village because it is time consuming for them, when they have a lot of work in the fields. Plus they can feed themselves without having to go to the village. Please, they are as much your friends as mine."

"Fine, but you won't do it. I'll go myself. Trust me!"

She finally nodded and walked silently to her room. without a word, she entered and walked to her open window. At this time of year, it was nice to feel the cool wind rush into the room, then slide through her unbraided hair. At that moment, with her fists closed, she breathed deeply to try to calm herself in the darkness.

She loved this little place under the window that her mother Caroline designed especially for her. She installed a sofa that Lia adored since she was a child. Sometimes she spent hours looking at the stars immersed in her daydreams like she used to as a child. She loved the glitter, the purity that emanated from them. It was the only place that allowed her to calm down during difficult moments.

Lia sat on her sofa as usual, looking up at the stars and meditating. John, for his part, sat on her bed, observing her for a few minutes. He decided to not to bother her and instead plunged into his thoughts.

Lia broke the silence.

"What's going on?"

"The hour is serious but not unstoppable. For the moment, there is no need to worry."

"Does this have anything to do with the sudden arrival of the Northmen?"

"It sounds like it's more complicated than that, but for now, we don't know more than what you learned tonight."

Someone knocked at the door. Lia answered with a weary look, suspecting that it could only be Nanou, her nanny.

"Yes, come in," with a complaining voice.

Nanou returned and waited for John to leave.

"Take good care of her, Nanou!" he turned and smiled at Lia. "For the moment, there's no need to panic, okay? When I know more, I'll come to you."

"My Lord, there no need for a lady to be interested in the problems of men."

With these words, Nanou closed the door to him. She put away the things around Lia's room, then approached her.

"Lady Lia, you have to sleep now!"

"You can go, I'll be there in a few minutes."

"Good! I'll come and check that you've fallen asleep."

"You mean watch me!?"

Nanou sighed and left. At times, Lia thought that her life choices did not correspond to the criteria of this family and even less to that of a young girl. From a young age, she had felt different, the only one in her family who wanted to understand and explore life around her. Sometimes she thought she could find answers that the world kept secret. More than once, she wanted to run away to find the path that would fit her. And not the one that was made up for her.

Being the only blonde in the family, she wondered about this physical aspect. She bore little or no resemblance to the members of her household.

Her brothers reassured her that it didn't matter. Although Lia was very close to them, her doubts gradually disappeared. And she became aware that the bonds she was building day by day were more important than her questions.

Today, another worry came to her. But this time it was a suspicion that concerned her entire family. There were rumors about the people of the North, treacherous and cruel people, who captured for the sake of torture, then raped women and children in front of their families and friends. Fearless and disloyal, it was said that the villagers were not much better. The war was over, but it did not make the fears, the hatreds, and the racial differences disappear.

As for *the Colombier* domain, it had become, thanks to her father, a place of peace. Lia was grateful to him for allowing her to live in a serene environment. Despite his harshness, he maintained a climate of peace in the villages that belonged to their domain. A comfort that few people could enjoy. Lia sometimes forgot this reality, and distorted it, aware that life was much more difficult in other lands. Yet she still dreamed of living in a world that knew neither fear nor distrust. Lia was a fighting woman and she would never give up, despite the narrow life of the women of her time, who only had to exercise their role as mothers. She believed that the family should not be a burden for the woman and that she should be allowed to be more free in her duties.

For the time being, her choice of life was impossible, but Lia hoped that one day she would be able to change things. Now she was fighting to be herself, the person she wanted to be, even if it was at the expense of her feelings for her parents. She didn't want to wake up one day with the weight of past regrets.

Tonight, Lia's sadness was great because she knew that she had to obey. It was important and she understood that. When her brother John looked so serious, it meant that he was very concerned about something, and the problems that could arise were likely to be life-threatening. Lia reassured herself that this was not her first punishment, but it was likely her last. As she lay on the sofa, she tried to convince herself that it would pass quickly. As soon as her eyes closed, her slumber was haunted by nightmares.

The punishment

A week had passed since Lia was forbidden to leave the house after lunch hour. She found herself going down to the living room to stretch her legs. The monotony of her days was beginning to weigh on her. Georgina was lying on the floor, drawing. Despite her young age, she was very talented. She was able to draw with precision whatever she imagined. She was also able to trace pictures from memory. Her mother Caroline and her two sisters were busy with their crochet work. Her mother looked up at Lia and said.

"Well, who's there?" she paused for a moment, and smiled at her. "It's good to see you!"

Lia returned her smile and sat down next to Georgina. She enjoyed watching her at the beginning stages of her work, trying to imagine the shapes she wanted to represent.

"This morning, when I woke up, I remembered our childhood memories," Ayana said, smiling at Lia. "Do you remember when we were children? I must have been ten and you twelve? We often had fun hiding in the woods. Do you remember that strange boy? I don't remember his name."

"I remember him well," said Lia in an amused tone. "He was the nephew of one of our servants. He came to spend the summer with them."

"We didn't lack imagination. Like that time we were fighting with your friends again, Monica! We were hiding and spraying them. I can still see their faces. They were so arrogant. They thought it was our father's hawk that was flinging its feces."

They all began to laugh.

"You know," Monica explained. "I never really liked them. I was so bored with them. I prefer to have fun with you."

"If we had known, we could have had fun together," Ayana exclaimed.

"That's in the past now. We had good times together. That's what matters," she paused, laughing. "Remember when Georgina tried to cook last year? It ended in a food fight."

"When Eliad tried to interrupt the commotion, he was surprised and finally gave in. It was the best moment of my life," Georgina exclaimed.

During the whole afternoon, they laughed heartily together, sharing these good memories. All these anecdotes made Lia smile again and allowed her to forget for a while about her uncertain future.

But soon after listening to her sisters talk about their future Lia's anxiety rekindled. She felt different and could not conceive of this way of life to which she was bound. She had to marry a man of high status and, like her mother and soon her sisters, have children and take care of daily life.

After this pleasant moment of exchange, everyone had gone back to their own thoughts. Suddenly, Lia realized that Georgina had completed her drawing. It showed a slender man with pointed ears. He had blond hair and blue eyes.

"Who did you draw?"

"I don't know. I just had it in my head. I was inspired by the stories that Nanou tells us at night. The legend of the Peoples of the Earth, the elves."

"You have a beautiful imagination. It is very well done. But why an elf? In the stories, they are vile and they have caused wars."

"They remind me of you."

"Me? Do I cause problems?" Lia said, smiling mischievously.

"I think they have understood that life is precious, that we must not destroy it, and that everything around us is sacred. This allows us to be in harmony with ourselves when we know how to respect what surrounds us. Perhaps they are superior because man destroys everything to obtain wealth and prosperity.

The elves are like you. They only see the best in everything."

Lia smiled, bearing her short nose and high cheek bones, hugging her tight. Georgina was touching and dreamy. Lia loved her innocence, and the way she created her imaginary world by taking what was around her. Lia thought that one day her sister would be able to draw wonderful pictures.

Lia looked more closely at the drawing, lingering on the facial features. She couldn't explain why she was so attracted and intrigued.

"Do you think I can keep it? Of all your drawings, this is the one I like the most."

"Of course, if you like it so much," she handed it to her, grinning, then stood up and kissed her. "I'm going to go see Thomas. Today he has to train. He's learning how to hold a weapon and ride a horse with our brothers. I don't want to miss this for anything. Especially since this morning, he bragged about how good he is. So I get to tease him if he fails, and I know he will," giggled Georgina.

"Honey, don't be so mocking with your brother," her mother cut her off.

"So what? He does it!"

"Come on. There must be other ways to react to show him your pain."

She shrugged and asked Lia if she wanted to go with her. She agreed. A little fresh air would do her good. She placed a kiss on her mother's cheek and left.

"See you later, sweetheart. I'm glad you stayed with us," as she stood up, she added. "Wait! Leave me this drawing, and I'll put it in your room. It would be a shame if it got damaged."

She gave the drawing to her mother and left with Georgina in the direction of the training grounds.

The camp was quite large. It housed the horses, an area for shooting practice, and another for fighting. Their brothers were already there. Samuel was teaching Thomas to hold his sword properly. Everything involving war came naturally to Samuel. Their voices were distant shouts over the landscape.

As Lia approached, she realized that Thomas was already beet red and clenching his jaw.

"Thomas, it's time you learned to listen. If you continue like this, I will stop, and you will learn alone."

Thomas pouted, released his fists, and gave in. He wanted to be better than his brothers so badly that he swallowed his pride. Finally, Lia and Georgina arrived and climbed over the wooden fences.

"Hi girls," Alexander greeted them.

"Hi! So Thomas, how are you doing?" giggled Georgina.

"Mock me, but at least I'll know how to hold a weapon one day, and I'll be there to protect you."

"Maybe, or one day I'll be able to learn, and *I'll be much better than you*!" responded Georgina with pride.

"I already know one sister who can beat a guy," John winked at Lia.

"Georgina, get over here! Take that gun and show us what you can do," Alexander interjected.

"With pleasure," throwing a glance of a challenge to Thomas.

Georgina was doing well. One day Lia caught her playing with wooden swords, and from that day on she decided to give her some advice. She took a sword and defended herself against her brother John, and managed to outlast Thomas. Lia applauded and encouraged her.

"Well done sis, show those boys that a girl only needs herself to protect herself!"

They burst out laughing. Her brother Alexander nudged her shoulder to tease her and said with a smile.

"That remains to be seen!"

"Let's stop! Thomas needs some serious training," Samuel told them.

"A little fun doesn't hurt," joked Alexander.

Samuel remained silent, and watched them work for a while in good humor.

After an hour of sword training, they headed to the horses. Today, he needed to learn how to ride a horse. Thomas couldn't figure out how to stand on a horse and hold the reins. They joked about it all afternoon. Even Samuel and Thomas were having fun, and Lia suspected that Thomas didn't understand on purpose. Finally, it was time for lunch, and they had to go home.

John stood beside Lia.

"You seem to be having fun today."

"Yes, staying in my chamber and watching time pass by is not really helpful."

"I couldn't agree more."

They arrived in the dining room, where their father was writing, as usual, not caring about his children. They all fell silent when they saw their serious father.

Some evenings, the meal hour went on without a word. It was really unbearable. Only at the end of the meal did George suddenly look up.

"So, Thomas, how did your training go today?"

"Good," he replied with wide eyes.

"Well, is that all? The first time your brothers held a weapon, they talked about it for hours. And you are just a *good*?"

"I mean, it's harder than I thought it would be, but I like it."

"Good, good. So Samuel, what do you think?"

"He will eventually learn, like everyone else."

"I might have learned more if Georgina and Lia weren't here," Thomas replied, feeling belittled by his father.

"What do you mean? Georgina, you know very well that I don't want you to bother your brother. He needs to learn, and there's no need to make fun of him."

"Yes, Father," Georgina was upset about being put down in front of Thomas. He would not fail to taunt her after the meal.

"And as for you, young lady," he glared at Lia. "When I told you not to meddle in matters that do not concern you, that also applies to men's affairs!"

"I just looked!"

"You know I don't like it when you answer me!"

Lia got up and left the table. Her father wanted to catch her and perhaps punish her further, but her mother held him by the shoulder.

When she got to her room, she immediately regretted spending time outside of the four walls of her room. Everything she did displeased her father. Everything was an excuse to put her down, and she didn't understand why he was so hard on her. She finally went to bed exhausted with anger. She fell asleep thinking about the drawing that Georgina made that her mother lost before bringing it to her room. For the first time in a long time, she had a nights rest without nightmares.

5

The sentence

The next morning, Caroline sent Ayana to pick up Lia from her room for a family meal.

"Come on, do it for me. I miss you!"

"I'm sorry Ayana, but I can't." Lia objected

"How stubborn you can be. Put your pride down and come with me. We'll be together. I have so much to tell you. I would love to have my sister by my side." Ayana pleaded.

Lia reluctantly agreed, wanting to please her sister. Ayana reassured her.

"Anyway, Mother asked Father to ignore you so that we could spend a moment without dissension."

"I'll be there in a few moments," Lia added, picking up a dress that was lying on the sofa.

"Thank you!" chirped Ayana and surprised Lia by hugging her tenderly.

Ayana detached herself from Lia and walked out with a smile on her face. Lia hurried to get dressed and headed for the stairs without much haste.

They were all there. When Lia arrived, everyone greeted her except her father. As usual, with his stern eyes riveted on paperwork, he didn't even look up for a second. The meal was quiet. Lia hardly spoke, preferring to listen, thus avoiding any bellicose discussion.

As soon as they had swallowed their last mouthfuls, a man rushed in. As if nothing had happened, his father continued his meal, grabbing his glass with his large hands. Without showing any interest.

"Sir, excuse me for disturbing you. We caught a man this morning trying to steal cattle. He does not belong to the Colombier, but to the estate of the Castle of *Massigny*. We arrested him and put him in the dungeon."

"Thank you! You may withdraw," he said stoically and calmly put back his glass without showing any emotion.

The Castle of Massigny was an estate not far from the Colombier, the city of Gemme. It was ran by Faley Isaie and his wife Faley Constance. The state was much smaller than the Colombier. Isaie is a close friend of George, and makes an effort to trade with each other and promote their domain. Caroline was friends with Constance. They saw each other often.

The girls knitted together over tea, but it was Lia who preferred to stay with Isaie.

Isaie was passionate about horses, and he had taught her a lot about them, like how to ride them and how to train them. But the most fun was learning how to tame wild horses.

Lia watched her father. Everyone was waiting for his reaction. It was not forgivable to steal, to lie, or to kill. It was punishable by death.

Georges Leusire was very attached to these values. As for Lia's mother, Caroline, she deplored this violence, not accepting it, but understanding the fact that someone had to act for political reasons. When a king or an heir pronounced a sentence, only he had the power to execute it.

When George Leusire took a life, he used his sword, whereas others had much crueler ways of doing so. Some cut off the hands of thieves and the tongue of liars, and for killers or traitors, it was both the hands and feet before finishing them off. Lia did not accept taking a man's life for any reason, but she appreciated that her father respected life and was quick to take it.

"Alexander, send a letter to Isaiah Faley! Ask him if he wants to punish their subject himself."

"I'll take care of it, Father" while hurrying to stand up.

"Why wait? He stole on our land," Samuel's words were sharp and quick.

"Maybe, but as nobles it is important to support and consider each other. This thug is one of their subjects, so it is our duty to inform them so that they participate in the sentencing. It is called respect! We will know more tomorrow. Let's go and rest" George bellowed before standing to his feet.

Just before leaving the room, he bent over and kissed Caroline on the forehead. Lia's head hung a bit lower than when she first entered the room. *"Why did I come to dinner?"* she asked herself. She was apprehensive about watching this man die and knew she could not avoid it. When a sentence was passed, all members of the household of legal age had to witness the death penalty. Only Georgina and Thomas, who had not reached the required age of twelve, would not attend.

Everyone had resumed their activities. Only Lia and Ayana were still at the table. When the guard announced the imprisonment of this man, Ayana became pale and disturbed.

Like Lia, she was reluctant to do this, but no one could change the course of history. Lia wanted to know more.

"What's wrong, Ayana?"

"I will go and rest. Suddenly I am tired."

Lia caught her by the arm.

"It's not just that, is it? Is it the sentence that puts you in this state? It's not the first time! So what's going on?"

"Well..." she let herself fall on her chair. Her hands were shaking uncontrollably. "That boy who was arrested, I have already met him. He is the brother of my beloved François."

"I didn't know you had someone. Why didn't you tell father and mother? You know they wouldn't have minded seeing you with a farmer when father himself married our mother who had no title."

"Do you think that today he cares? Times have become harder and it is his duty to marry us with an heir. Otherwise, the king would not accept it and father could lose everything."

"Mother wouldn't let him. We are righteous enough girls to keep our reputation." Lia said softly, taking her sister's hand.

"Not only that," Ayana was so angry that she was on the verge of tears. "He and his family are on the run. People from their village discovered that François was an adopted child, born in King Leon's territory. He was just a newborn when they found him around Arrow. Despite this, no one wanted to keep the secret, and because he came from another territory, they wanted to kill them." Ayana began to whimper, "they are considering them traitors. They managed to escape and I haven't heard from them for a week. When they find out who he is, they will start looking for the others."

She collapsed, and Lia took her in her arms. Interdict, she did not say another word. So much of the history was sad.

"We need to talk to Mother about this." Lia insisted, clenching her fists.

"Why? She can't do anything!"

"Maybe, but she might talk to father. We never know."

She nodded and Lia went looking for her mother. In the hallway leading to her room, she heard voices. She hid to try to learn more. Her father was talking to a guard at Massigny Castle. In the distance, Lia could hear,

"Sir, the prisoner you are holding may be a fugitive, and we must interrogate him as soon as possible to find out where his family is."

"How could you know so quickly that a prisoner was being held?"

"We have been tracking him for several days now."

"Good. Make yourself at home, if you have any problems, come to me!"

"Thank you, sir."

When he was far enough away, Lia rushed to her father. Maybe if he knew about Ayana, he could help this family.

"Father, please stop him!"

"What are you talking about? It's none of your business. Go back to your room!" he said in a hoarse voice, which would usually have scared her.

Her mother arrived at the same moment. Lia continued with more conviction hoping that her father would listen.

"The family they are looking for. There is a man Ayana is in love with. If you have a little heart, do something!"

"You don't have to teach me how to run a kingdom. You have to accept the facts no matter how painful they are. You have to get used to it!" his voice thundered.

"We're talking about feeling, not power. If you want, you can send someone you trust and scare them away."

"Young lady, you don't know what you are talking about."

"I am talking about justice and not about the act!"

"Sometimes we just can't. Do you know that the young man in question is not from here?"

"Yes, but he was found as a baby. A BABY!" she wailed. "He grew up here. He is part of our land. He never even knew the territory of King Leon. All of this is ridiculous!"

Her father sighed, admitting that there was some truth in what she had said.

"I agree. But imagine for a moment that I do what you ask. If the king hears about this story, our whole family will have to answer for this treason. Some situations are unfair, but I have no choice. And it is better that it happens this way. If they find out that your sister had an affair with this man, she could be condemned too, and I won't be able to do anything. For that, I will speed things up. He will die quickly. I can promise you I will send Eliad."

Eliad was very close to the secrets of the family and was always involved in the important tasks. He did not have children and never wanted to get married to enjoy life and women. This may make him insensitive to certain tasks, but his deep values make him an honest and loving man for those to whom he is devoted.

"It's not fair. He didn't do anything!," Lia dropped to her knees, although she wanted to run into her father. "They were just in love! Since when is that a crime?"

"Since belonging to a kingdom is important, I cannot change anything. By doing so, I am protecting you," he paused for a moment before continuing. "You will understand one day" he said before stepping down.

Lia wanted to catch him and explain to him that there was only one possibility, but her mother prevented her from doing so.

"I know it's hard but he's right. You can't control everything." Her mother said deeply.

"But this is horrible. Ayana will be devastated," Lia wailed.

"We'll be there for her," her mother placed her hand on Lia's, "Where is she?"

"In the living room," Lia answered regretfully.

"Let me talk to her. Go rest. You need it."

Lia watched her go. Helplessly, she wondered how she could regain her composure when she thought that the sentencing would take place the next day, taking with it the fateful fate of a family.

The next day, she woke up with a sinking feeling in her stomach. Ayana must have been in a bad state. With no appetite for breakfast, she preferred to go and find Ayana in her room. A guard was posted outside her door.

"Madam, you can't go in. Lord George is speaking with Miss Ayana."

Lia waited in the hallway with a lump in her stomach. He had to tell her about the previous day's events and, as usual, remind her of the duties of the ladies of the castle. She had to attend the execution no matter what the sentence was and above all to hide her pain.

A few minutes later, he walked out, looking at Lia without a word. She entered on the fly, discovering Ayana crying on her bed over the death of her love. Lia looked at her helplessly, then lay down beside her, holding her in her arms, when their mother arrived.

"Ladies, it's time," she sat down next to Ayana. "Your father told me about François and his family. My love, I am sorry! Life is unfair, but your duty is to stand by your father."

Caroline invited them to get up, and they left together for penance. Ayana, walled in her silence, and did not cry anymore. Lia felt sorry for her. Her pain was too heavy.

Their father was there, with the guards of the castle of Massigny, who the leader, Faley Isaie had not been able to come, but his wife Constance was there to represent him. Caroline sat next to him. As for his daughters, they sat next to their brothers.

Immediately the protocol began. The guard of the Castle of Massigny stated the sins of the prisoner, which with regard to Lia, were not.

There was a crowd to see the execution, people from the castle of Massigny as well as the denouncers, although the latter should have stood in the place of the accused.

Lia looked at her sister when the prisoner entered the courtyard, but she showed no emotion. There was nothing on her face. She was mute. When they finished tying him up, her father came down from the platform, and a guard gave him his sword. From a distance, her father looked impressive. His broad shoulders gave him more presence, which made him more ferocious.

At that moment, Lia grasped hands with Ayana, and their father executed him. Ayana ran away from Lia.

Lia ran behind her sister. After catching up with her, she spent the rest of the day by her side. However, no amount of comfort could ease Ayana's pain.

***

A month passed, and Ayana now acted as if nothing had happened. When Lia tried to talk to her about it, she told her that it was a mistake and that there would be other suitors for her.

Since that day, she never spoke of it again. Everyone mourned in their own way, and Lia hoped that one day she would forget and be happy again.

6

A nice surprise

Six weeks later, after Ayana's love tragedy, Lia found herself confined to her room. She suffered the imprisonment, where the daily routine forced her into servitude.

As soon as she woke up, someone came in on the fly. Nanou, while rushing to clean the dirty linen, took a hurried tone.

"Sweetheart, it's time to get ready. Your brothers are already at the table. You have a surprise today. So stop dawdling! Eliad is waiting for you outside."

With these last words, she left, slamming the door behind her. Nanou entered the room every morning, bustling about without Lia saying a word. She got along with her quite well, despite her imperious and narrow-minded character. She had raised every girl in this house. Now she was more concerned with Georgina because of her young age, but still spent a lot of time with Lia trying to teach her good manners.

As for Eliad, it was not a torment to have him by her side, because Lia got along with him very well. Master of arms of the domain, he had taught her brothers how to fight.

When he caught them teaching Lia how to handle a weapon, he preferred to take over and teach her himself, without her father George knowing. He was very fond of Lia. He had even confided to her one day that if he had had a daughter, he would have liked her to look like her. Eliad and her brothers taught her everything from holding weapons to fighting, but she also excelled with the bow and javelin.

At the moment, her brothers were not very concerned about her, they were too busy with their father. She couldn't stand being treated like a girl and being left out. As for her sisters, they spent their time embroidering for the future posterity of the village.

Every year, a feast was organized to gather the villagers. It was their father, George, who started this tradition, and they were the only village to do so. George organized this event to bring people together despite the difficulties the country was facing. It worked very well, and everyone looked forward to it. There was drinking, gambling, and dancing without worrying about tomorrow.

Although Lia enjoyed the party, she was still frustrated by being confined. She spent her days in the gardens behind the house, where there were many acres with a wide variety of flowers. Her mother, Caroline, had embellished the place with her care of the plants and her taste for decoration. She had learned everything from her grandfather, who had passed on to her his love of flowers and his natural gift for preserving them. Lia enjoyed watching her garden.

When she wasn't spending time in the garden, she was walking down a random path lined with white trees. The fallen leaves dotted the path like a white tablecloth. One of them led to the different enclosures that George had made to raise many species of animals. About thirty species lived at the back of the manor, some of them were particularly ferocious.

In the Leusire family, animals were loved more than people. The animals knew all the members of the Leusire family very well, and some could only be cared for and fed by them. Georges wanted his children to learn responsibility at an early age.

So, from a very young age, he asked them to choose which animals they wanted to take care of and these became theirs. Thus, as soon as they could walk and talk, each of the siblings was given the task and the chance to raise and feed the inhabitants of their own enclosure. He said that this was fortifying for future life and if one of their protégés died because of lack of care, he held them solely responsible for their actions.

George had the peregrine falcon, Caroline the servals, Samuel the lions, Alexander the tigers, John the wolves, Monica the cheetahs, Ayana the leopards, Georgina the bears and Thomas the wild dogs. As for

Lia, she was in charge of the hyenas. All of them were very attached to their animals. It would be impossible to separate them without one of them suffering.

Lia had five hyenas in her pen, one male, two females and two newborns.

Sometimes, certain species were allowed to spend a moment outside their cage but only in their keeper's presence, and one at a time, so as not to disturb the domestic animals. It was customary for the inhabitants of the Colombier to see members of the Leusire family in the company of exotic animals.

Spirit, Lia's dog, was very playful with some animals, so she often took him with her.

That morning, she hurried to get ready, left her room and walked down the hallway to the dining room.

"Hello, Eliad!" she said happily.

"Good morning Lady Lia!" stopping her in her tracks he said, "Today, you are to have lunch in the main room."

"Why is that?"

"You'll find out soon enough!" he said with a mysterious tone.

They walked down the hallway to the reception room on the other side of the house. Lia's parents used this room to organize sumptuous dinners in due form, welcoming leaders or prestigious friends, which the girls were not allowed to attend. Apart from that, there were a few times when Lia had lunch in the presence of her family and close friends in this room.

That was probably why the lunch was held in the reception room today, or the dining room was too busy with party preparations. When she entered the room, she saw her brothers sitting at the table. Someone grabbed Lia immediately, sweeping her up into their arms.

"Oh my darling, it's so good to see you again."

"Auntie Jeanne, what a pleasure!" she said, hugging her back.

"And what about me, don't I get a hello?" her uncle Victor came to interrupt this embrace.

Lia then turned to her paternal grandparents, Leonard and Louise. They gave her a quick wave of the hand as they turned away from her as quickly as possible. Lia was not very close to them, they were not very warm, and one could say that they had a bilious temperament. After the greetings, everyone took their seats at the table.

"So kids, do you still have those funny animals?" asked Uncle Victor.

"Of course, Uncle. Mine is all grown up and if you want, I'll gladly take you to see them," replied Georgina.

"Pfff, your father has some funny ideas sometimes. I say that you don't raise kids with animals, it makes them more temperamental."

"Oh Sir Leonard, it didn't stop me from growing up well. Look at the result," said Samuel with his best smile.

"It depends, for whom, my dear," replied Grandma Louise, looking at Lia from the corner of her eye.

Although Lia was no longer surprised by their derogatory remarks, she was still hurt by them. Unlike Thomas who disrespected his elders and to whom they never said anything to, Lia always respected the people around her.

What was the point of entering into conflict? They did not understand her assertive ideas. This was the reason they gave her remarks and made a difference about gifts and affection on each visit. Although they did not give her hugs and kisses, they used to pat her brothers and sisters gently on the head, except for Lia.

Her brother Alexander noticed Lia's saddened look and didn't wait for any further remarks against her to start a new conversation.

"Get ready for this year. Mother and the girls have prepared a beautiful ceremony. Now that I think about it, girls, where is mother? I didn't see her this morning."

"She had to wake up early today because some of the preparations were late. Besides, I'll be leaving you now. I have to join her. Georgina and Ayana hurry up! Lady Louise, will you come with us?" asked Monica, hurrying to finish eating.

"With great pleasure my children, let's go so that I move these old legs."

"If you don't mind, I'll go with you too. Are you coming Lia?" chimed Aunt Jeanne.

"No, later. It's my turn to go feed the animals."

" Well, see you later my little one," smiled her aunt.

Lia returned her smile and watched them leave. She got along very well with her aunt and uncle, whom she admired. Her aunt Jeanne had never been able to have a child and she considered Lia her own. As for her uncle, he had the same spirit as her. He wandered from village to village and gave his support and know-how to whoever wanted it. But what Lia admired most was that they loved each other as much as they did on their first day of marriage. Shouts in the room drew Lia's attention.

"No I don't want to!" yelled Thomas aggressively.

"Let's see Thomas. You have to study to be a good guy. Look at your brothers!"

"First of all, you're not my father so I don't listen to you."

"That's enough, Thomas. You're going to go with your uncle, come on!" replied Grandpa Leonard sternly.

"I'm joining father. He needs me to finish preparing the meeting. Will you come, Sir Leonard?" interrupted Samuel.

"Of course, it's even urgent, stop dawdling! Thomas will go to the study room immediately and you will listen to your uncle. Have I made myself clear?"

"Yes," he breathed out in a vexed tone.

This was the first time Lia had seen her younger brother so docile. The reason why he was never contradicted was based on a family secret. It turns out that when he was born, he should have died and her parents were so deeply marked by this event that they were always tolerant of him.

Now only Lia and her brothers, Alexander and John, were left. She took advantage of this time away to find out more about what was going on.

"Now that we are among ourselves has anyone heard from the people of the North?"

"No sis, I promised you I would keep you posted," responded John gently.

"Relax and enjoy. The party is about to happen," said Alex, half amused.

"Easy to say. You have the right role, you are not blamed all day long and you can come and go as you please."

Alexander thought about it and tensed up.

"You know, we are not always aware of everything. Samuel, the heir of the Colombier, is obliged to be present at all these meetings to which we are not often invited. But when it comes to war, that's another matter. As Samuel's brothers, we are his adjutants. Be confident. We are not preparing for a future war. This is more like a border dispute for which our dear king reminds us of our duty."

"Maybe you're right Alex. But believe me, those northerners we met last time weren't there to mark any territory." Lia continued her theory, "What if there was a war going on without anyone knowing? What if they were there to recruit? I'm sure a war is coming, and as usual, the small villages will be the last to know and the first to go into battle," said Lia.

Her brothers did not respond and considered for a moment what Lia had just said.

Alexander broke the silence.

"Well, sis, don't worry if it turns out the way you said, you won't be the one sent to war. And as long as we're under King Theodore's rule, there won't be any women on the battlefield," Alexander said with a half-smile.

"If that's how you hope to reassure me… Anyway I have to go, the animals are waiting for me."

Lia got up and headed for the door, when her brother John held her by the shoulder.

"Wait, don't you know the best part? Father has given us his blessing for you to accompany us into the village this afternoon."

Lia looked at them, they were both smiling. Lia was surprised but happy. She jumped on John's neck and kissed him.

"Hurry up and feed the animals. We are leaving soon."

She nodded as she ran to the pens, passing her uncle Victor.

"Why are you in a hurry," he grinned and walked towards her. "Do you mind bringing me with you? I would like to see your animals."

"If you want, but today I take care of my brothers' and sisters' animals and my own, because father is allowing me to accompany my brothers outside the Colombier."

"Ah... And what are you going to do about it?"

"I don't know and I don't care. Today nothing can make me happier than to go to the village."

"And what are you going to do?"

"I have a lot of things to do. I'm going to see my friends and the villagers. I think that if father agreed so easily, it's because he knows that it's me who will be confided in. It has been months since the incident at the tavern. The Northmen have never returned despite their warnings. I think he probably finds this strange and is sending us to investigate."

"I see, my little one. You know, even as a young girl, you had a way of making people trust you. If anyone can learn anything, it's you."

They arrived at the main enclosures, Lia entered, and one of the hyenas who was not sleeping came to meet her.

"Tell me Lia, do you think I can get in?"

"I'd rather you not. They are wild animals, and one bite can kill you. My brothers and I can approach them. We have raised them since they were born. We are part of their family. If anyone else enters their enclosure, they will feel threatened and will attack immediately. Especially since the one next to me is the crowned princess of the group, which makes her the most aggressive."

Lia began to feed them. Then, she came out of the pen and watched them with her uncle.

"Why is this female white?"

"Usually hyenas are striped or spotted. One snowy day, I found her, alone, in the forest. She was still a newborn. At first, I didn't see her, because, as you can see, one could be mistaken when it comes to her white color. It was her cries that alerted me. Since then, I have always wondered if our paths were destined to cross. I never found another like her" Lia's eyes were glaring into the field. A faint smile lifted her high cheekbones.

"Did you give them names?"

"Their names appeared to me as evidence. The leader is Neige. She is special to me. We created an indescribable bond, since I saved her."

Her uncle watched them for a moment, only the sound of the hyenas disturbing his thoughts.

Suddenly, he snapped out of his reverie.

"Well, well, I must leave you. I'm going to join your father. The meeting probably has already started, and as usual, I have to be late. See you when you get back?"

"Without fail!"

Lia headed for the other pens and hurried to finish. She was just making her way back when she heard voices coming from the hay shed. She approached and recognized the voices of her uncle and Eliad. She stood behind the door to listen.

"At the end of the party, I will talk to her. I have to tell her the truth. No one has the right to hide such a secret. It's her life," Victor exclaimed.

"Maybe, but your brother will surely not think so. For him and madam Caroline, moreover, this secret seems to be of primary importance for the future. They consider that it would be too dangerous to tell her."

"I don't agree with them, especially at this time. Lia is old enough and smart enough to understand that."

At these words, Lia stiffened. Now they were talking about her and a secret. She concentrated more on the conversation to know a little more about what they were hiding from her. But they were talking lower and lower, and the words became more complicated to discern.

"I'll talk to her after the party and no one can talk me out of it," added her uncle. "Are you with me? Will you keep this secret?"

"I agree with you entirely, and I'll keep quiet," he replied, shaking his head. "Quiet... I think I heard a noise, don't move."

Lia hid behind an oak tree. She saw Eliad come out and survey the area, and then her uncle came out. The two men looked at each other, exchanged an inaudible word from the oak, and then went separate ways.

She waited for a little so as not to find herself in the path of one of them. A thousand questions were jostling in her head. She was worried, wondering what could be so serious that they could hide it from her.

She came to her senses. For the moment, there was no need to torment herself, because her uncle would talk to her at the party. It was only a matter of patience. She started to run because her brothers were not going to wait for her forever.

7

The Molière

*T*he sun was already high in the sky when John, Alexander and Lia took the horses to the village. Lia was right. They had to find the villagers and find out what had happened to the Northmen. They had to find out where they went and if they had returned as they had predicted.

"I hope we don't learn anything unpleasant," says Alexander.

"I hope, above all, that none of the villagers will have given in to the threats of these men," added John.

"Who would blame them? For the most part, they have never held a weapon in their lives. The scythe is the closest thing they have to a weapon," said Lia.

"Sure, but enlisting with them would be worse than death," Alexander says.

"Finally, what exactly do we know about these Northmen, other than gossip," John wondered.

"Right, but the aggressive tone of the last time makes me say that everything is true," Lia worried about it.

"Would you doubt this war, John?"

"No, but this war is nothing more than a desire for power in which we are dragged in despite ourselves. The most intolerable thing is that it is always the same people who are attacked, even before our dear king does something." A group of birds flying over the treetops interrupted them for a second, emitting shrill sounds.

"Don't talk about our king in that tone of voice anymore! Do you realize that if a malicious ear were to wander in here, you would be taken prisoner, tortured and killed for slander? Think of your family suffering the same fate for harboring a '*slandere*' as they say," said Alexander aggressively, leading his horse through a narrow passage, where the sun was barely hitting.

"Calm down, I know it. And if you have to hold your tongue!" Alexander looked at him again. "It's okay. I'll calm down. We've arrived anyway," responded John with a silly smile.

They were approaching the town when suddenly a villager blocked their path.

"Who goes there?" looking at them more closely, he exclaimed. "Oh lord, I didn't recognize you. I apologize!"

"It's nothing. Why are you so suspicious?" said John.

"I'm sorry, but those men," he stammered in a shaky voice, looking around. "They came back yesterday, and waited for almost an hour, beers in hand at the tavern. You know that everyone here likes Mr. Leusire, so no one followed them. Everyone barricaded themselves in fear of reprisals. Although your guards were present in case of rebellion, we were not reassured by the rumors.

"What rumors?" interrupted Alexander, when suddenly a gust of wind made the horses nervous.

"Haven't you heard? There are rumors that King Hilarion has raised the Black Army. If that is the case, we are lost. Please understand. Despite our attachment to this village, we could do nothing against them!"

"Don't dwell too much on legends by definition they are myths and nothing more. There is nothing to fear from them, and if there is, no one is indestructible, not even them. They will taste the iron of our swords, as will every enemy that faces us. Well then, are they gone?" Alexander asked impatiently.

"Yes my lord, after an hour spent in the tavern, then walking the streets of the village to show themselves, they finally left on their horses. But that is not what worries us most, my lord. Last night, the village was awakened by screams. Your guards are missing, and some children as well. All that was found were scraps of flesh and the head of one of your guards, left on the ground, further into the woods."

"Is that what scares you? There's no need to be fearful. They took you by surprise. They're just cowards, and cowards shouldn't scare us. Don't worry, I have a plan. Gather the village. We have to talk to you!"

"But lord, it is not the men of the North who frighten us, but those who killed your guard. He was not killed by a sword! His body was torn apart, his head was ripped off, and I swear to you that it was not a human who could have done such a thing."

"Well, I'll see for myself," John replied. "I'll meet you in the village," he said, turning to his brother.

Alexander nodded and watched him go.

"Meanwhile, gather the villagers! My sister and I will stable our horses," said Alexander urgently.

As they walked into the village, where everything seemed inanimate, Lia realized that her brother was worried, so they continued and entrusted their horses to the village squire. When he finished tying the horses, hurried footsteps could be heard in the distance. Once they were alone, he turned to Lia; nervousness and insecurity were all over his face.

"Let's wait for John. He shouldn't be long now, and I want to know more about this case. After talking to the villagers, I would like you to go to the tavern to get people's opinions, then join us in an hour."

"Okay. How bad do you think it is? What are they afraid of? Is it what the legends talk about?"

"We don't need to worry. I think they were just trying to scare us. But this case disturbs me, especially since children are involved. You shouldn't be concerned about the legend. It's just a kid's story."

"I hope we find them in time. You will track them, right?"

"Yes, and that's why I'm going to take a group of men. I'll leave right after I talk to them. You go back with John."

"You'd better take John too. What if the villagers were right? What if it was something much more important?" petitioned Lia, while looking at him with concern.

He looked at her with a tender smile and took her by the shoulders.

"Don't worry little sister. I won't leave you in peace anytime soon! Besides, John needs to report to father, who wouldn't be happy to have you come in and do it for us. Unless you want to spend your next year locked up. Either way, I'm afraid it's too late. Someone should have warned us before. They should have left our territories long ago. They are excellent horsemen."

Lia pondered her words, thinking of the sadness that the parents of the missing children must be feeling. While both of them were deep in thought, John arrived disconcerted.

"What's going on, John?"

"I think our villager was right. I've never seen anything like it. It's not a normal death," he said breathlessly.

"Do you think it could be an animal?"

"Maybe. His marks are more like those made by bears. But what seems curious to me is that the body was torn apart but not eaten. What animal would leave its prey? Especially since we can see that the thing that killed, deployed a superhuman force."

"So no worries! It's probably an animal. These northerners must have bred them for war. And that's why they kill without necessarily devouring their catch."

"Probably, but I'm still confused by it all," John said darkly. Silence fell between them leaving only the sound of agitated leaves from the wind gusts in their ears. With each second, the wind howled stronger and stronger.

They remained pensive, their faces tense, all of this history worried them. When Lia was little, Nanou used to tell them stories before going to sleep, legends and stories about monsters. Lia had never wondered if they could be true.

At that moment, she caught herself thinking about the possibility of some truth, although it was unlikely and she didn't really believe it. Even though she had already found out the hard way that life sometimes offers surprises.

They headed for the town's guardhouse. The building was old, but overlooked the whole village, as it was well placed and elevated. The village was not very big, because only the merchants lived in the village, while the others had their houses in the surroundings. Although the village is old, it was quite well maintained, which proves that Georges Leusire brought prosperity to his village.

The guard house also had the function of announcing some news, who people were gathered. So when approaching the place, it was not surprising to see the gathering of the villagers. But what was surprising was to see almost all the people of the Moliere gathered like a herd. Most of them fearful, looking around, others—probably those who had lost their children were devastated by grief.

Alexander climbed onto the stage.

"People of the Molière, I gather you here in this dark hour, for I have learned the sad news and I am deeply touched. I am planning a search in the forest for survivors and, in the best case, the pursuit of the Northmen, if they are still around. I ask for your support and as soon as possible, because by the time we get back to the Colombier we will lose precious time to find the survivors. Those who are able to hold a sword should join me immediately. I will also need a tracker to spot the tracks. I can't do it alone. So who's coming?"

No one raised their hand. The assembly was silent until one of the villagers spoke up.

"What is the guarantee of survival? They are probably already dead. I apologize to the families for their losses, but you, Men of the Colombier, are safe within your walls. We alone suffer fear and terror. Last night, where were you? Why didn't you go to face the dangers? They are gone and that is all that matters," he said sharply.

John joined Alexander and took over the speech in a firm voice.

"Listen up! I know you're scared. We are all scared, even us. We, too, are not safe from danger. We risk our lives for you. If no one fights today, then we might as well give ourselves up to the Northmen. If there is no hope, then why live? Yes, why do we live? Of course, we were not here last night, but we stayed up late to set up a safe zone. We asked our king for help and he responded. By the time the party is over, we will have members of the royal guard here. In the meantime, we have to rely on each other, as we always have. Let us continue to support each other. We are strong together. They are unarmed in front of an assembly so let's take advantage of it. They are only a dozen, and we are much more. What do we risk? Yes, I know the legend scares you. If it is true, remember that it can only act at nightfall. We have time. So it's now or never!"

John's speech made an immediate difference, and you could see that he had touched the most hesitant. But no one moved, except one, the best hunter in the village.

"You are right, my lord. We have always fought for peace. Your father protected us well, and it is for him that I follow you and for our peace," he said bravely.

At these words, a handful of men approached. Alexander signaled the blacksmith to bring weapons.

A few minutes later, about twenty men left with Alexander in the lead.

When he could no longer see Alexander and his men, John stepped down from the stage and walked toward Lia.

"Do as Alexander tells you. I must report to our father. I'll come back for you in an hour," said John, breathing heavily.

Then he left to get his horse. Lia went in the direction of the tavern. On the way, she hardly met anyone. While people usually greeted her, today they rushed home, closing their doors violently.

After a few minutes, only the wind surprised the quietness of the end of the day. Lia thought she would find no one at the tavern, but she was wrong. When she went inside, there was no room for anyone to sit down. The innkeeper saw her and beckoned her to come closer.

"So little one, what are you doing here? You better go back home, you will be much safer."

"I have to wait for my brother John," she said with a determined tone.

"Hmmm, I must admit your brothers are brave. Look at your brother Alexander. Who knows if he'll come back?"

"Stop talking nonsense!" she growled. "He will come back, as will all the others."

"I wouldn't be so sure if I were you!" said a man beside her sadly. "What happened last night still gives me the shivers. You all heard those screams. There was nothing human about them."

"Stop talking!" replied another. "You drink too much, and you must have been delirious, that's all! I heard the noise and it was nothing more or less than an animal noise. You Leusire must be used to it, right?"

"For sure, but I wasn't there. I can't say anything," responded Lia.

"I can!" said a bearded man who couldn't even stand upright. "As far back as I can remember, men told of having seen evil beings. They said that they came at night to steal children and to eat them. They are tall, and black, which makes it easy for them to hide at night. Most of the time they walk on all fours ... and can crawl on the walls as fast as a bolt of lightning. In one night, they can destroy an entire village. And most of all, their screams can terrorize whoever hears them, to the point of insanity."

"In this case, old man, we have nothing to worry about, since last night's screams were nothing more or less than grunts," someone shouted aggressively, accentuated by alcohol.

"Careful, kid, I've heard those growls before and I can tell you that was just the beginning. That was just a warning, next time it'll be a lot worse," he said darkly.

The old man had just terrorized half the tavern, including Lia. A melee ensued about the disagreements that had occurred the night before.

Two hours had passed when John came to pick up Lia. They took the horses to return home.

"So sis, what do the villagers say to each other?"

"They are all scared. Not all for the same reasons, but they are afraid, and this is already creating great tension. An old man spoke of an ancient legend about monsters, terrorizing whole villages to kill anyone and eat children."

"He's an old man! Most become unbalanced with age. He must have mistaken wars for monsters so don't worry. There is no such thing, or our beasts would be monsters."

They preferred to joke about it and laughed like children. But Lia's questions remained, leaving her perplexed. What could kill and kidnap so many guards, without leaving any trace?

"Hey John, can we stop by Kéo and Rose?"

He smiled at her.

"I had thought of that. It is also possible that they saw or heard something, since they are quite far from the village. When I went to warn them, I had asked them to pay attention over the next few days."

"If something happens, Kéo will know. He is an excellent tracker and an even better hunter than you!" she said mischievously.

"I'm not as sure as you, sis. Be careful what you say," he said, half laughing, half amused.

They were approaching their friends' house when Rose came to meet them.

It was a pretty little cottage surrounded by the forest. Their pasture and garden were further north, where the forest ended. Flowers surrounded the place, which made the modest dwelling more pleasant to view.

"Hi, you two. I bet you're here because of the events of last night, are you?" She took in the sight of Lia, "did your dad give you permission to go out?"

"Yes, for today only! I will be grounded again when I get home."

"I'm going to look for Kéo in the field. Come in and make yourself comfortable," smirked Rose.

They left their horses at the stables and waited by the fire. A few minutes later, Kéo entered abruptly, driven by his anger.

"When you warned us to be careful of what might be going on, you didn't tell me it could be so dangerous. Next time, don't ask me for a favor! I work hard for a living, and my wife could have been killed with your nonsense. What could I have done, alone and unarmed, eh tell me?"

He had moved closer to John, his fist raised. Lia had never seen him so angry.

"Take it easy," said John smoothly. "If we had known what was going to happen, we never would have put you in danger. You know me, don't you? We've been together since I was eleven. How could you think I'd want to hurt you?"

Rose put her hand on his shoulder, and Kéo calmed down almost immediately. He took a seat and lay down.

"Sorry, but last night I was terrified. We could hear screams in the distance coming from the village. It was crazy," he said frantically.

"It's strange... Nobody alerted us. If we hadn't come to the village, we wouldn't know anything about it and those poor children..."

"I can't imagine worse," Kéo said. "When I went to the village this morning to see what had happened, I found the elder on the platform warning the inhabitants, or scaring everyone, I should say. In fact, he even made everyone promise to keep quiet, and not to warn anyone because it could make things worse until we were all killed."

"This one, my father should have locked him up long ago. He's a drunk, that's all!" John said wearily.

"I would have come to you to warn you but I was on my guard and I didn't want to leave Rose alone," he said, putting his face into his hands.

"Don't be sad! You did what you had to do!" he said, with a cajoling voice. "what happened last night exactly?"

"I don't know. After I heard screams, I went out and started heading towards the village, through the forest. I heard footsteps, so I hid. Then, I heard guards, I couldn't understand what they were saying, and children were screaming. The guards were all killed, their bodies were torn apart and carried in bags. I just heard something like, '*They were taught a good lesson. If they knew what attacked them, most of them would have killed themselves first.*' They walked away to the north. The kids... I couldn't do anything. I was alone. How could I? Maybe I should have tried."

John stood up and put his hand on his shoulder.

"You have no reason to blame yourself. Who could have done anything? To act would have been madness. You would have been killed. Don't worry. Alexander went to see if he could follow a trail. Did you see any beasts or anything that could have decapitated those men?"

"No, nothing."

"Thank you! One more thing, could you show me the place where they went. I'd like to take a look. Hopefully, they left a track."

"I'll take you there!" he said, getting up quickly.

"Stay there Lia. I'll be right back."

They went out leaving Lia alone with Rose, who was busy making good cakes. She was an excellent cook.

Rose had not always lived here. She remained evasive about her village of origin being in the South. As for Kéo, he was very mysterious. We didn't really know where he came from. He only said he was an exile from the North. John and Lia were the only ones who knew this secret.

John had become friends with Kéo when he was younger. Despite their age difference, they became very close. Kéo taught John and Lia a lot.

On Lia's fifteenth birthday, John allowed her to accompany him to meet them. She immediately hit it off with them. Kéo taught her how to survive in a hostile environment and Rose, who was very selfless, confided a lot to her.

At first, they had difficulty integrating into the community. Both of them were very different from the others, and at the beginning they were distrusted, but then they showed their usefulness and their integration became gradual. Over the years, they have become pillars of the community.

While the boys were looking for leads, Lia asked Rose about her recipe. An hour later, they heard them return.

"We didn't find anything." he replied to Lia sadly. "We will return. Thank you for your help Kéo."

"Let me know if you hear anything," said Kéo.

He nodded and left, followed by Lia. On the way, they did not say a word. The day had been exhausting both morally and physically. All that did not let augur anything good.

At the Colombier, the evening was agitated. The girls were frantic about preparations and the men were on the warpath. Alexander and John spent more than two hours reporting to his father, and from the look on his face, he was not happy with the result. He had Lia call him to tell him what she had heard on her side, before sending her back to her room without any thanks, which hurt her feelings. John caught up with her on the stairs.

"It was nice to have you around. You know, father is preoccupied, as usual. He's being tough, even with us. Try to get over it." he said, trying to comfort her.

"As if Father was showing his feelings at all. I thought I'd get used to it over time, but as I get older, it gets worse. I don't know how you do it. He pays more attention to Samuel than you do," she turned around quickly to hide her tears.

Once in her room, Lia slumped on her bed and fell asleep.

Let the party begin

*T*he day of the party arrived. Lia did not want to get up. Nanou entered on the fly, without bothering to knock. She immediately brandished curtains and party clothes.

"Aren't you ready yet?" she said stiffly. "Hurry up and help us finish. We all got up early, but as usual you only think about yourself."

She closed the door quickly, without Lia being able to retort. Not really in a hurry to join the preparations, she took her time. The day would begin with a simple but elegant outfit. We would play and attend the various feasts. At the end of the day, a more formal and festive outfit would be in order, to make way for dinner and dancing. The party would last late into the night to allow those who came from afar to enjoy it.

Lia put on a short floral summer dress, shortened above the knees, and a pair of ballerinas. She put on light makeup and tied her hair in a ponytail.

Finally ready, she rushed to the main room where many household employees were working in the four corners of the garden to finish installing the last bit of details. Nanou saw her approaching.

"Here, Lia, I see you are ready. Now take this to the buffet and make yourself useful. There is still a lot to do," said Nanou squeezing into the kitchen and coming back as fast as she left.

Hardly, loaded with holly and candles, Lia was pushed in the direction of the west garden and was immediately dazzled. This year they had outdone themselves. The main entrance was entirely decorated with lanterns. The bridge that spanned the river and led to the field was beautifully decorated with flowers. Hedges of bushes, embellished with lanterns, ran from the house to the animal shelters. The day's buffet was spread out all along the main path, which was an amazing area.

The tables were nicely covered with a white tablecloth dotted with red petals. The path was white, and all around the fields, there were games, a place for dancing, and benches for rest.

When evening arrives, we will swap out the décor and replace it with white tables and chairs decorated with red bows.

Everywhere, lights and lanterns would light up this garden with a thousand colors.

Caroline, her mother, helped decorate the tables.

"My darling, here you are at last. You look amazing! Your presence means so much to me."

"It's a pleasure to be able to join the party. It means so much to me too," smiling at her mother.

She hugged her tenderly, and Lia continued.

"You and the girls have done a beautiful job, it's just wonderful!"

"Thank you," glancing around. "I don't know where your father is. I hope he gets here in time!"

"Is he still on the case?" asked Lia interrogatively.

"Surely, he is waiting for the generals. But let's not talk about that anymore. We have a party waiting for us. Besides, be nice today. We have someone to introduce you to," Caroline said, smiling at her.

"Please! You know I don't like it, but you're persevering anyway," Lia gasped. "Just the idea of imposing this arrangement on me, revolts me deeply. Whether I like it or not!"

"Stop being silly, otherwise, you will end up alone or your younger sisters will start a family before you. I only ask you to be nice and kind. Do this for me!" she begged.

Lia took a deep breath to show her displeasure, but she knew her mother would not let go until she agreed. She nodded her approval, then left to finish the preparations.

Lia was annoyed. She wondered if her mother would ever stop introducing her to potential suitors. Every year for the past three years, on the day of the

Molière festival, her parents would take the opportunity to introduce her to a man. Lia would pretend to be interested in him and at the first opportunity, she would leave him alone. Very often, the young men, full of themselves and with excessive self-esteem, would show themselves to be distant afterwards, although her mother would beg them to try their luck again.

At the time Lia was reprimanded, but it never lasted long. Her parents knew deep down that love cannot be controlled. They, too, had had a lot of trouble getting others to accept their love. They wanted their children to be happy. Lia did not feel available for love. Not at the moment. Even though deep down she admitted to herself that it was fear that guided her choices. Only the love of her family and friends was enough for her, and filled her with happiness.

Moreover, with what had just happened, she was concerned for their safety and that of the people of the Molière. She worried about it every day, so love took a back seat.

She joined her sisters to help them finish the preparations. She approached Monica, who was making the bouquets to put on the tables. This last one addressed a disdainful moue to her.

"To what do I owe this mood? Have I done something wrong?" Lia asked irritably.

"No, but you are always absent for important moments, especially when you are needed," she said sharply.

"That's not true! I'm here for you," she growled.

"Where have you been for the past few weeks? Where have you been when we've been worrying about getting the party ready?" Monica continued aggressively.

"Is that why you're mad at me? You know that father has unjustly punished me!"

"But you're not helping anyone by acting like this, and father was right. These days you only think of others outside of the manor. You seem to forget that your family lives here."

"One day, you won't live under this roof. You will have your own family. Should I sacrifice myself thinking only of others and deny my principles, just for you?" said Lia in a heavy voice.

"You are acting selfishly, that's all! I am here for mother. Are you?" her voice had become increasingly sharp, almost strident by the anger.

"I'm not as impressionable as you are. You have your own codes and I have mine! If you, my sister, don't accept it, maybe we should stop talking!" said Lia turning around and trying to keep down her anger.

"I think so!" responded Monica.

She left, bouquets in hand, leaving Lia furious. As they grew up, they gradually drifted apart. Monica lived according to the doctrines imposed on women, which was very far from the diktat of Lia's life. With time, they respected each other with a certain limit. Lia loved her sister very much, but as they had opposite characteristics, they often quarreled over nonsense. They were both stubborn and proud. They enjoyed spending time together, and they had decided to make an effort to speak frankly to each other and never let their resentments get the better of them. So far, it had worked; they were coming back to each other more easily. And it had been a while since they'd fought. Lia was saddened by this quarrel.

Her sister, Ayana, had heard them.

"Don't blame her. She blames you for the distance you put between us," Ayana said, trying to put down the situation.

"I understand, but why such a reaction?"

"A few months ago, she was dating Tharsile, a member of the royal guard."

"But they are not allowed to have a wife. They must be devoted to the kings," said Lia with surprise.

"I know, but one day when she was in the garden where he was waiting for father, he confessed his feelings to her. At first, Monica was taken aback. Surprisingly, she confessed to having the same feelings. They made their vows together, hiding from the world. But, a week ago, he broke up without saying anything. She is devastated by pain, and I think she would have wanted to tell you. She wanted you near her, but you locked yourself in your room every time she came to you, refusing to talk to anyone."

"How could I have known?" she said defiantly, but mostly sad by her own reaction.

"You've been so closed off. Lately, it's only Alexander and John that matter," said Ayana calmly.

"Although I'm sorry, a crush is less important than what's going on," she continued defending herself.

"That's what we're blaming you for, putting our feelings after what's going on, which, by the way, we have no idea about. Whereas Monica, her feelings are real, and she is suffering, no matter what happens in the world, we have to stick together, right?" she said carefully.

Lia was silent for a moment. Her sister was telling a part of the truth that Lia found difficult to admit. Things were different when Ayana lost her love months ago, and she has changed so much since then.

"I agree that you are right, but what is done ... is done."

"Maybe if you went to see Tharsile to find out the reasons for this breakup, it could already be a first step and especially allow Monica to move on," hinted Ayana.

"And how do you know all this? I thought they wanted to keep it a secret?"

"One day, I caught them hiding behind an embankment. I promised not to say anything, anyway, it would have been inappropriate of me, given..." lowering her eyes in sadness.

Lia smiled at her, and put a hand on her shoulder. Lia admitted that lately, she wanted to make a difference by trying to help, and she forgot that her sisters needed her too.

"And you, how are you?" said Lia.

At this question, her sister's face lit up.

"I can't wait for the party to start. There's a cousin of the Faley family who is coming. And, from what I hear, he is charming."

"Either way, it's not like we are short on men tonight," Lia said amusingly.

"There is more," she blurted out frantically, "from what they say, this cousin will receive a supreme status by the king! I can already see myself on his arm walking towards the king." They both laughed, then she added, "By the way, mother is introducing you to someone tonight," half amused.

"So it seems," answered Lia without much conviction.

"Come on, maybe they'll finally pick someone interesting this time."

They looked at each other and went into a fit of laughter, guessing in advance that this could not be the case. Their parents had never understood their taste in men.

"Lia, you come with me to the kitchen. I have to finish helping to make the cakes. I know you like to do that."

Lia followed her, and for a few hours they made chocolate cakes, cookies, and other pastries for the day.

The time of the party was approaching. Guests were already arriving before the appointed time, a sign that they were eager to escape it all. Lia saw Rose and Kéo and went to meet them.

"How are you two doing?" Lia asked them with a big smile.

"We are exhausted. It is difficult to sleep," Kéo admitted.

"I understand. I hope that our problems will be resolved quickly."

The crowd stopped talking when George and Caroline appeared on top of the bridge to announce the opening of the festivities. Caroline began the speech.

"Thank you for always being present for this celebration. My family and I are happy," she motioned to her children to join them, "to welcome you each year to our estate. We have carefully prepared this day full of surprises. As you have already seen, we have come up with a few changes to the decorations. I hope you like them. It's just the beginning."

She raised her glass. Shouts of joy followed her gesture. Then, George had to make a speech about what he had learned concerning the Northmen and their attacks. There was a sense of anticipation on everyone's faces, a search for answers to the questions everyone was asking. Already, all eyes were on him.

"Dear inhabitants of the Molière, I know you have been impatiently waiting for my speech. I have heard your words and understood your fears. These last few days, I have worked hard to bring you an answer. Unfortunately, I do not know more than you at the moment about the people who kidnapped our children. In spite of this sorrow, I am happy to see so many of you gathered here before me. Tonight you will be at my table with the royal guards. You will be the first to know of the measures taken by your king. I promise you that we will find our children and that the culprits will pay for the pain they have caused us and for the death of our soldiers. If it is any consolation, we have had guards and trackers out beyond our lands for several days to see if they can find their tracks. If any information reaches me, I give you my word that I will keep you informed. For the moment, let's try to have fun but above all to take our minds off things because we need it. I understand that it is not easy, but complaining will not change anything. This year, let's be united in this sorrow. Together we can grow and overcome. To that end, let's try to enjoy this day and have fun for those we have lost. We also celebrate this holiday for our deceased. May those in the afterlife hear our laughter and find peace. TO THEM!" he shouted the last word.

Everyone raised their glasses, shouting. George was a good speaker. He spoke so well, that you could already see people more relaxed than when they arrived.

The music started, some began to dance, and others approached the buffet.

Being a good hostess, Lia passed from guest to guest and ensured they didn't need anything for more than an hour. She was having a good time, dancing and eating in good company when her uncle Victor joined her and offered her a drink.

Since the beginning of the day, she had been anxious for him to talk to her. So she followed him without hesitation.

"What a pleasure to be here, your family is so important to me," he paused. "You know I'm getting old and at times I look back on past choices with regret. But they are there and I can't change them. I hope you won't make the same mistakes I did. Lia, do what your heart tells you. It doesn't matter what people believe or think. Only you can make your life good."

He stopped talking to look at George. He looked so sad, and it saddened her. She didn't know what had happened.

"Don't worry, it's okay. It's just a little nostalgia, that's all," he replied to Lia. "Your dad is a good person, even if you can't see that he loves you. Everything he does, he does for you. Remember these words, if you ever doubt where you came from. Your parents love you."

"Uncle Victor, is everything okay?" Lia said concerned.

"Truth is a treacherous word," he continued talking, "it can distort the meaning of life, the truth is good but I hope that for you it will not make you doubt who you are. You know the important thing is not how you come into the world but what you choose to do with your life. It doesn't matter who you are, as long as you believe in yourself. And in the people who made it possible for you to become the person you are today. Your greatness of heart and strength. Never forget that, my little Lia."

As he was about to speak to her, her mother, Caroline, interrupted them.

"Sorry to interrupt. Victor, would you forgive me if I borrowed her?"

"Of course, Caroline," turning to Lia with a wink. "We'll finish our conversation later."

He smiled at her and walked away, leaving her furious. Her mother had just ruined the entire end of the day to introduce her to her current suitor. Lia was desperate to have a secret kept from her, and even worse, to have it revealed to her.

Her mother pushed her toward a young man. He was thin as a bean, brown hair, blue eyes, and was rather effeminate.

"Desire Ursula, I present my daughter, Lia," forcing her to come closer.

Taking her hand to kiss it, "Nice to meet you, my dear," Desire smirked.

"I apologize, I have to leave you. I have a reception to hold," exclaimed her mother cheerfully.

"Please, Madam, with me, Lia is safe," he said bravely to impress Caroline and Lia.

Lia rolled her eyes, convinced that she was probably better at swordplay than he was. As she walked away, her mother looked at her, waving and cheekily grinning.

"If you don't mind me saying, you look great tonight."

"Thank you," she said, noticing that he waited for her to retort with a compliment as well, but in vain.

"You know that I have very rich lands. Unfortunately, my father died when I was four years old, and he left me all his possessions. My wealth is by far the most important, without offending your father, of course and…"

She stopped listening to him. As usual, he was a fool and full of himself. Lia was bored to death. Like the previous ones, he only talked about himself. Thinking she had made enough effort, she excused herself on the pretext that she was needed in the kitchen. When she arrived, Rose was helping to serve the desserts.

"What are you doing here? Enjoy the party. You don't have to do that," Lia was much calmer, and her voice was much softer than usual. "Your mother seemed overwhelmed, and I just offered to help. I don't mind. what are you doing here? Aren't you supposed to be with a nice young man?"

"Charming? He is the opposite of charming!"

"Of course, still unable to make efforts," said a male voice

Samuel had just entered the kitchen.

"Easy to say, I'm incapable of loving someone by force. You could understand that," she said sharply.

"No, I can't understand it. I am going to marry a woman who has been suggested to me."

"I, too am incapable of understanding," Lia said curtly.

"I think about our kingdom and the good it will bring to the Colombier. I am less selfish."

"You're exaggerating, and I don't run a kingdom! What do you care if I don't marry him? I'm just asking you to appreciate that I'm happy, and by marrying him, it wouldn't be!"

"You two, that's enough!" Rose snarled at them. "Let's enjoy the party, shall we? I don't think your mother and sisters did all this wonderful work to have it ruined by childishness."

"You're right Rose. I'm going out to have fun," Lia looked back at her brother. "I am more and more saddened that you are becoming as stoic as father."

Then she went out. On her way to the games, she saw Tharsile, alone on a bench. She took this opportunity to call him and keep her promise.

"I'm sorry to bother you. I'm Lia, daughter of Leusire George."

"I know who you are," he stopped her. "Nice to meet you. We never had the opportunity to speak."

"You must have been too busy with my sister," said Lia, as quickly as possible.

He became white and very embarrassed. He did not know where to put himself.

"How? Did Monica tell you?" he was beginning to turn red.

"More precisely, Ayana, but anyway, Monica would have told me eventually. We don't have many secrets between us. Don't worry. I won't say anything."

"Thank you," said Tharsile with relief.

"I don't have all the bits and pieces of the story. But I would like to ask you a question?"

"I'm all ears."

"Why did you break up? She still loves you, you know."

"I know," he lowered his head. He looked so sad. "I had no choice, one of my brothers-in-arms saw us. He swore to me that he wouldn't say anything if I stopped seeing her. I had no other choice. What could I do? This story would have led to nothing. I am chained to my vows. I hope I have your word. Otherwise, my life ends here." He got up quickly and walked away, glass in hand, leaving Lia perplexed and sorry.

This had not advanced to anything. Lia could not admit to her sister that he still had feelings. Knowing her sister, she would persist and it would end in tragedy.

She decided to finish the day enjoying the party. She joined Alexander and John, who invited her to dance with Georgina. She didn't think about anything—nothing but to have fun in the presence of her own loved ones.

9

Fire and brimstone

People invited Lia to dance, and she was having a good time when it all started. It was late, and most people were having dessert. After the first scream, everything went very fast. Lia's mother grabbed her by the shoulder.

"Listen carefully to what I am about to say. Our lives depend on it. Run to find Georgina and Thomas! When you find them, meet me at the back of the castle. If it ever … if it ever gets too dangerous, run. I want you to promise me that," squealed her mother.

"What? No, never!" she said alarmed.

"Please! Promise!" closing her hands tighter.

Lia had never seen her mother so terrified and angry.

"I…" Lia quickly glanced around, watching the panic on everyone's face, "I promise," she said looking deeply into her mother's eyes.

"I'll get your sisters, now go," she kissed her like it was the last time that they would see each other.

She ran like never before. No one had seen anything coming. Hundreds of men entered the garden, killing some, torturing and assaulting others. Lia felt helpless. She had never been so afraid. But she had to find her family. Getting them to safety was the most important thing to do.

She ran, calling out their names, and glancing around. They could be anywhere. In the distance, she saw her uncle bending over a body, her heart stopped beating, and she ran with all her might. Her uncle was clutching her aunt, who had been stabbed to death in the chest.

Faced with this awful scene, Lia also began to cry. The death of a loved one is the worst thing on earth, especially when the life is snatched away from him or her in this way, so unjustly. Her uncle was devastated.

"Uncle Victor," said Lia smoothly. "Don't just stand there. I know it's hard, but we have to keep going. Quickly!"

He found it hard to let go of her, although Lia couldn't blame him, because she too, found it hard to let go of her in this way. But they had no choice but to run.

They moved away, but pain prevented them from hurrying. Suddenly, two men rushed at them. They grabbed Lia, but her uncle pushed them away with a volley of punches. Her uncle was beginning to find himself in a bad way. Using a statue that was within reach, Lia jumped behind them, managing to disarm them and kill one of them.

The second man reacted quickly, grabbed Lia by the arm and gave her a blow. She fell, stunned and vulnerable, at the mercy of her attacker.

Two others arrived and hit her uncle, who was also on the ground. They beat him severely. As her uncle lay on the ground, as if dead, one of the men took a knife and, with an amused look, struck him several times in the abdomen. He must not have known how to do it because he did not die immediately.

Her uncle's tormentors were no longer amused, so they approached Lia and pulled her by the hair toward the woods.

Suddenly, Spirit arrived and leaped at the men. They tried to fight back, but their fear got the better of them, and Spirit jumped at the throat of one of them while the others fled. He didn't die right away, but grabbed his throat with his hands to keep the blood from flowing, took a few steps before collapsing and finally choked to death. Lia struggled to get up. Spirit tucked his muzzle under her armpit and helped her walk.

She was beginning to lose hope. Everything around her was burning. Just as she was about to give up, her mother came running.

"My love, I'm here, come on, let's go!" she grabbed her, gently as much as possible in that hurry.

"No. Wait, I couldn't find anyone and Victor…"

Her mother looked toward the lifeless body of her uncle Victor. She turned to Lia and stroked her face.

"Come on. There's nothing more we can do. I found Thomas and Georgina," she sniffled.

"Are they all safe?"

Too weak, stunned by the blows and the shock, Lia fainted. When she woke up, they were in a cart. Her dog was lying at her feet, her mother beside her. When Caroline noticed that Lia was awake and trying to sit up, she helped her upright. Lia's head was pounding from ear to ear, preventing her from seeing her surroundings right away. Her mother sighed and asked her,

"How are you? You've been sleeping for a while"

"I only have a headache," she touched her head as if to find a wound, to put her thoughts back in place.

Looking around, she realized that in the cart were only her mother, Georgina, and Thomas.

"Where are the others? Where are we going?"

"We're going to the Faley's," Caroline was trying to escape the conversation.

"Will the others join us there?"

Her mother did not answer immediately. Instead, she looked at her with a crushed expression. Georgina and Thomas began to cry.

"No, no one is waiting for us, only us," she squealed almost in cry.

"What do you mean? I don't understand!" Lia stammered, trying to stand straight.

"It's just us. I couldn't find your father or your brothers. They must have gone into danger and I don't know, my dear... As for your sisters, I arrived too late. They were kidnapped. I couldn't do anything. Then you collapsed," she said deflated.

In shock, Lia did not respond immediately. She took her mother in her arms. She had never witnessed her cry like this before, which made her realize the gravity of the situation. She began to cry in turn.

She stood up, looked at her mother, and said.

"We have to go back, and help them. We can't give up. This is our family!"

"To do what? You want to send Georgia and Thomas, your youngest siblings, to face them? That's crazy. You must accept the situation, even if it's insurmountable," she beefed her teeth.

"How dare you give up? Don't you love them? Wasn't it you who taught me never to give up on those I love? That was just talk, wasn't it? You're just running away. I don't want to be like you!" she said frantically.

"You're not speaking with reason my love. We're alone. Love can't always be strong enough. For the moment, I think of you. We give up a battle but not a war."

"So what's the point of fighting if we don't do anything now?"

Lia turned around and cried alone. She felt unhappy and exhausted. Her mother landed near Georgina and Thomas. The sun was high in the sky when they were approaching the castle of Massigny, like a greeting, small birds singing their songs on their way, came to disturb their thoughts.

No sooner had they passed through the castle gates that the tension began to build. The guards, standing at attention, let them pass, only after checking their identity. As for the maids, they were running around the courtyard waving sheets and food. Although the castle was smaller than the dovecote, it was well-kept and decorated with so many flowers that one could hardly see the walls.

Caroline got down from the cart. At that moment, Constance appeared at the door, and came forward to embrace her.

"We got the bad news just as we were about to come to the party. I'm so sorry," pushing her inside. "Come in and stand by the fire."

Inside, Lia lay on the sofa while Constance fed Georgina and Thomas. Her mother, Caroline, had gone to the kitchen, to let herself cry some more without being seen. Lia tried to fall asleep, but the scenes of that awful night kept repeating in her head. She was crying her eyes out. In a few seconds, all had been taken away from her. The pain tore at her chest, and she felt like she couldn't breathe.

The next morning, after a restless night, she entered the kitchen. Two maids greeted her, and urged her to have breakfast, although she didn't feel like it.

She was in her thoughts when suddenly two arms embraced her. It was Georgina.

"I'm so scared," admitted Georgina.

"We are safe here."

She took her in her arms not knowing what else to say. She was just as frightened as she was, and just as lost. They ate in silence and followed the servants who had prepared a bath and warm clothes for them. Lia chose practical clothes, a black spindle and a black tunic, and braided her blond tresses.

She was more determined than ever to return to the Colombier to fight.

In the living room, she saw her mother.

"I'm sorry about yesterday. I got carried away."

"Please my love, don't apologize. Come here," she took her in her arms. "We'll go somewhere safe, she released her embrace to look into her eyes. I'll have some things to tell you when we get there. I know a place no one here knows but me. But you have to trust me and follow me. I can't tell you anything until we get there."

"Look, Mom, I have to talk to you too. Let's sit down," Lia pointed to the chairs beside her. Her mother looked at her attentively. "I'll go back there. Maybe I'll find some traces that will help us find them. Then there are my friends, our grandparents Leonard and Louise..."

"What are you talking about? This is absurd and dangerous!" she stammered, shocked.

"I knew you wouldn't understand, but it's my decision and..."

"Before we go any further, there's someone in the kitchen you should check out."

Lia watched her mother curiously, then stood up and walked slowly forward. She hoped to find one of her sisters, one of her brothers or even her father.

Her heart was pounding and she hoped she was right. She pushed open the kitchen door and found Eliad sitting at the table. Tears came to her eyes and he took her in his arms.

"I'm sorry, I'm glad you're alive but I thought maybe ... well..."

"Don't apologize. I understand. I also wish it was a member of your family. Let's sit down, Lia. Here, have a glass of water. It will do you good."

Eliad's face was stern. It must be admitted that he was a person of little smile and rather serious, but he had never been so closed, so thoughtful. It was especially the first time that Lia saw him afraid. Lia waited for him to speak, she didn't dare disturb him and she was just as worried about what she might learn.

"When the assault began, I was with your father, your brothers and the king's guards. We were in the big office when it happened. We heard screams. At first we thought it was the drunkenness of the party, then we quickly realized what was happening outside. When we reacted, it was already too late. Your father and brothers tried to stop them. Tharsile and I were trying to find you. At the same time, your sisters were in a bad way, and your father was being surrounded. Tharsile shouted at me that he was looking after your sisters while I was helping your father. I don't know more about Tharsile. Your mother told me that it was too late. I'm sorry about that. For your father, I fought as best I could at his side. I was shot in the leg with an arrow, and then I don't remember anything. When I woke up, people from the village were treating me, and I came here as fast as I could, hoping I could find you. Oh, I don't know if I did everything I could, but I feel like a coward for failing to protect your family. Forgive me Lia," he put his hands to cover his face, devastated.

"You've already done a lot!" she put one arm around his shoulder.

They stopped talking, each one remembering the worst moments of that evening.

"This is probably not the right time, but yesterday my uncle Victor," when she said his name, her throat tightened, "wanted to tell me something during the evening. Do you happen to know what it was? She wondered if what was being kept from her had anything to do with this attack."

"What? Uh, let me rest and we'll talk later?" he tried escaping the question.

"Of course," she replied in disappointment.

She was about to leave when Eliad added.

"Your friends, Kéo and Rose left for Arrow."

"Arrow? But why?"

133

"I saw them get on a cart. I asked around. Apparently, the cart belongs to a merchant who does business in Arrow and with the events, he was going sooner than expected. They didn't want to stay any longer and I don't blame them. But if your friends get caught as fugitives... I'm sorry, Lia."

She thought for a few seconds, and announced her decision.

"I'm going to look for them. I know that at least they can be saved. I won't let them down. don't try to stop me," she said determined to save them.

"Then I'm coming with you!" he said, trying to get up with his weak body.

"No, you have to stay here, look after my mother, Thomas, and Georgina, for me, okay? With your leg, don't take it the wrong way, but you wouldn't be of any use to me."

"In that case, outside, you will find my bow and sword. Take them and your dog. I hope that he will accompany you."

"Of course, he could never leave me anyway," smiling at him.

"We'll be waiting for you. Be careful and remember everything I taught you."

"I promise!" she said, giving him a last hug.

Lia went out to find her dog and took up arms. She was determined to do something, and it was now or never. She took the path, preceded by Spirit, following the directions indicated by Eliad.

***

When Caroline entered the kitchen, Eliad was still sitting at the table

"Where is Lia?" her eyes darted around the room, searching for Lia.

"She is gone."

"What is it? What do you mean, gone?" each word trembled with realization.

"She went in search of her friends."

"What? But ... you let her go?" Caroline said defensively.

"Since when can we tell her what to do? She would have left at some point, and it's time for her to go her own way."

Caroline sat down, remaining pensive, then added.

"She still doesn't know about the secret?" He nodded. "It's better that for the moment she doesn't know," she said with a deep voice.

10

A completely different path

*L*ia finished telling her story from when the party was invaded to her reunion with Rose and Kéo again. Tears came rushing to her eyes, as she was unable to hold them back anymore. Rose took her in her arms, trying to soothe her.

"I couldn't do anything, nothing … and yet I feel so guilty. I lost them all, and I don't know if I will ever see them again … alive. I am lost. I don't know what to do or where to look." The deeper she went into the forest, the more fragrant it became; her sobs were drowned by the sounds of wolves howling in the pathless forest.

"Remorse doesn't help us move forward. We were there too. There were so many of them," Rose took Lia's hands. "One person can't save the world. It's a sad tragedy, but don't give up. We'll find a way to bring them back. I have learned from life, that as long as it is in you, you have no right to give up. Life is full of darkness and in those darker moments, you must also remember that you are not alone and that others are counting on you. Sorrows are a part of life. You have to be patient, and everything will pass. Bad experiences will become memories and you will wake up stronger and everything you have known will seem far away. You will be able to create new experiences from your past mistakes. In every tear there is a ray of light, and it is up to you to see it shine. We will find a way, I promise you. We are here for you," Rose reassured her as they was to their go to Massigny Castle. "Let's start by trying to find Caroline and your brother and sister. Then we'll go up to the Colombier. Maybe we'll find something interesting there," added Kéo.

"For what? Georgina and Thomas are traumatized enough. As for me, it seems painful to walk through what was once my home. Going back would mean that the world I lived in is gone. I'm not ready to accept that yet."

Kéo and Rose looked at each other skeptically, and discouraged. Lia could see in their faces that there was little hope of finding them all alive.

She stood up. At that moment, she was so overwhelmed with anger that she was ready to fight to the bitter end to find her people. She walked ahead of everyone forcing them to get up and keep moving.

Spirit trotted by her side for company. Isolation sometimes helped her find the hope to go on.

Many questions remained unclear. The men who had attacked the Colombier had certainly not come to look for allies. So there was something else. Something that her family possessed that aroused so much envy. When she found her mother, the questions Lia had been asking would have to be answered. To face the danger and save her family, she needed to know the truth.

They walked the green pastures of the forest for hours. Emile, who until then had not said a word, joined Lia and took her by the arm.

"We should rest, your friends are exhausted and I confess that I am too."

"We would waste time," she said candidly.

"Look, if we don't stop, I'm afraid Rose won't make it. She's on the verge of falling over from exhaustion. You'll find out the truth when the time comes. Let's try to get some rest. A good rest gives you a clearer head," he said as smoothly as possible.

Lia nodded in agreement. While her friends settled in behind a slope, out of sight, she went off to gather wood. Emile followed her, without saying a word.

They returned to Kéo and Rose fast asleep at a fire that they made on their own. Even half scared to death they were able to close their eyes but not Lia. Lia could not find sleep and preferred to watch the surroundings a few steps away from her sleeping friends. Emile came to join her and tamped the fire.

"It's hard to sleep when you're cold." Emile turned to Lia and sat down next to her, "Your family is lucky to have you. I've met many people along the way, but few have the same determination as you. You will fight no matter what you find in your path. I kind of admire that in people."

"I thought you liked being alone?" she answered, half in her thoughts, without looking at him.

"I like solitude, even if sometimes I dream of starting my own family. I wish to care for them as you care for yours." He looked at the sky, smiling, "a wise man once told me that my heart was made of stone. And that I would have to wake up to live." He turned back to Lia, looking down to catch her eyes "your story moves me and you intrigue me. If you accept it, I will go with you to search for your family when you are ready."

"Why me?" she said, surprised.

"I would feel guilty leaving you to your fate. I have a code, and helping people who are most affected by life, is one of them. I know what it's like to be alone, and I don't want anyone else to go through it, so if I can help, even a little." He paused for a moment, puzzling her, before continuing. "Tell me, before all this happened, did you have a lover?"

"You mean a suitor?" replied Lia, turning red in her cheeks at the change of conversation.

He moistened his lips, "yes."

"Of course not. Why?" she confided a bit on the defensive.

"I don't know. I'm interested," he smiled at her, pushing his hands behind his head. "Did you once have suitors?" he asked gleefully.

She suddenly started laughing, and explained.

"Every year we would have a party and my parents would introduce me to a man they had chosen. But, of course, it never worked out. I don't like to be forced into anything, especially when it comes to feelings. Most of them were so cheesy and so arrogant, and that's not what I'm looking for."

"If I may say so, at first sight it is difficult to understand you. You are not ordinary. You are pleasant, but you seem to have this impenetrable, almost savage shell about you. What I have deduced is that you don't accept to be loved very much. Are you afraid?"

"Maybe. I am what I am. Love is as powerful as it is destructive. I don't want to be disappointed. Trust is something you have to learn. People think trust is easily earned, as if it means nothing. I don't believe that. When you love, you have to be patient," she admitted while staring at the stars.

"That's true, but you also have to appreciate the moments as they come. If we close ourselves off too much to protect ourselves, we end up not enjoying the present."

She smiled at the thought while Emile eased back to lay down and join her in admiring the stars for a few seconds before falling asleep to the sound of the soft crackling of the fire. She found herself alone in the middle of the night, enveloped by the distant howls of animals and the wind blowing through the leaves of the trees. Lia lay down, gazing up at the starry sky, wondering at that moment if any of her family members were also watching.

She looked at Emile for a few moments, and found herself thinking that he was a pleasant man, and she wondered if he was developing feelings for her. If he did, she admitted to herself that she would be flattered, because deep down she liked him too. She found him to be a keen observer and rather clever. She came back to the harsh reality that somewhere, her family might be suffering, while at this moment she dared to think of love.

She needed to find help. Perhaps negotiate with King Theodore, if he would accept to hear from a woman, or if Emile could pose as a servant of her family and go on their behalf? The questions swirled in her head and kept her awake. She finally dozed off, thinking the worst, and cried herself to sleep.

The next day, after resting for a few hours, they set off again. Kéo stood by her side. He had been thinking of what to say to keep Lia's spirit intact. He finally found the heart to begin talking to her by saying,

"You know, your brothers are fighters. I know they never told you about their adventures, but here's one that should make you smile. The answers you've been waiting for may not be coming anytime soon, so be prepared for any eventuality to avoid disappointment."

He took her by the shoulder and told her about their adventures, taking in a deep breath.

"One day, when we were on our way to Arrow to buy cattle, we met Chavallois Benoni and his wife, the Nobles of Gleenay of the *Goose* Castle. You don't know them well, but he is a very good warrior. He has fought many times with your father. They are not very good friends, because their points of view differ a lot, but you have to admit that he has always been there in case of problems. He is a man you can count on. That day, we walked the path together. He asked your brothers many questions. It was strange, and it was as if he knew something and was trying to tell us. It was almost like he was under a pact not to tell us. He asked how close you all were and if for some reason your brothers were to find out one day that one of you was not who you seemed to be or if it happened that one of you was not really part of this family, what would their reaction be? That day was the first time that your brothers, especially Samuel, let their emotions speak for themselves. They finally said that no matter where you came from, the feelings you had developed were much more powerful than the blood bond. Their family was the most important thing, and they wouldn't let anything destroy it no matter what cause or newfound truth. The only thing they were sure of was their love for their family. Strangely enough, many questions were directed at you. Samuel added that you were one of the few people who knew how to love life as it is. That you understand how it works when others only think they understand it. You revealed to people the world as it is, beautiful and imperfect. Though often troubled by the fear of rejection, you rarely opened your heart to people and when you did, you did so with purity. You have given them your love, and for that, they will fight until their last breath to protect you. Through these words, I understood how much they love you. I know how hard it is, but don't give up being yourself in this quest. They will never forgive you. Don't turn off what you are. You have a whole life ahead of you. They wouldn't stand for you destroying it to save them, especially if it's unattainable."

"You're asking me not to give up, but … ," she replied, crying.

She was deeply touched. It felt good to hear those words and it broke her at the same time.

"Think carefully before you make a decision. I know this is hard. The situation you're in is unimaginable, but let's try to consider all the possibilities before acting."

With these last words, he left to join Rose. Lia didn't know if she could give up without at least trying. It would haunt her all her life, that's for sure. She couldn't bear to live with such a burden.

The priority was to find her mother to find out more. She would then think about what is best to do, as always.

They had just arrived at the castle of Massigny, and no sooner had they passed the gates of the large courtyard than Constance rushed out of the house to come to them.

"Lia, you need to get out of here right now. You are not safe. Your mother and the others left two days ago. Guards from King Theodore came. They were looking for you. Apparently, you have been found guilty of treason. They managed to escape thanks to my servants, but the guards might come back. I don't know where your mother went. She gave me this message for you.

One day you will meet again to know what awaits you. For now, you need to get to safety. You will know how to make the right decision. You can't follow it, but the time will come when you will know everything. I'm sorry I can't do more, so sorry. Good luck Lia!

Kéo pulled Lia by the arm. She stood there, puzzled. Where had her mother gone? They stopped. Rose put her hand on Lia's shoulders asking her the inevitable

"What do we do now? Where do we go? It's not safe anywhere anymore."

"I don't know," Lia answered confused. She felt lost, more than ever. The situation had just gotten worse. "I don't know where to turn."

"I won't leave you," replied Emile. "I know a place where you'll be safe. I really think you'll get your answers, but in the meantime, trust me."

"What does that mean?" replied Kéo suspiciously.

"The mysteries will be cleared up when we arrive to where I am taking you," continued Kéo, answering as normally as he could.

"Who are you? What do you want? You are not here by chance, are you?" said Kéo stiffly to Emile.

"It's complicated, but trust me."

"Lia, I think we should go together, maybe talk to the king... Lia?" said Kéo annoyed.

She collapsed to her knees, holding on tightly to her head. The questions were exhausting her and ripping deeper into the wound within her heart. Although she was with Rose and Kéo, she felt alone. She realized that it was only with her family that she felt truly safe, and she was no longer there. She didn't know what to do, but she was sure she could trust Emile, no matter what he claimed to be.

"I think we should leave with Emile," Lia said, standing to her feet.

"Lia, we need to talk to each other and alone," said Kéo firmly.

"Make up your mind quickly. We're in the open here," Emile said while walking away to give them privacy.

"Listen, sweetheart," said Rose, "I think Kéo is right. Emile may have been following you all along. It's probably a trap."

"I feel that he can be trusted. If he wanted to kill me or even turn me over to the mobsters, he had the opportunity more than once. Look, I know you're scared. I'm scared too. But we have to stick together. You're all I have left. It may be selfish, but don't lose faith. Talk to the king? He'd kill us on the spot, without having a chance to plead our case."

They looked at her for a few seconds, then nodded.

"Let's stay on our guard. At the slightest sign, the slightest suspicious thing, we take our legs to our neck, you hear me?" said Kéo irritably.

"Understood," she answered them. Then she turned to Emile who seemed to be waiting patiently and said, "we follow you!"

Emile led them to a village that was a day's walk away. There he could buy horses that would take them to the coast, to the fishermen's village.

A deep poverty marked these villages. No one went to sea anymore, and there were just a few boats to fish in the open sea. The people of the village were too afraid of what might happen beyond the horizon. Some had sailed the sea to find wealth, but did not return, or others returned dead. Their bodies were found on their makeshift ships, dried out while others were all crumpled up as if something had absorbed all of the life out of them.

Samuel once told Lia about it. No one wanted to live near the water, the poorest were sent there.

So Lia was surprised at their destination. It would take them a little over twenty days on horseback.

The trip was strenuous. Lia spoke very little, preferring the presence of her dog Spirit over anyone else. Kéo and Rose, worried about the turn of events, speaking only to each other. Emile was hunting rabbits whenever they settled down in their makeshift camps.

Although they had traveled a long way, Lia was surprised to have finally arrived. Tired and morally exhausted, they had exchanged only a few polite words during the trip.

Emile gave the horses to a skeletal old man, who kept thanking him as they made their way up the hill.

After a few kilometers, he came to a mouth that opened onto a cove. In the middle of the water was a ship. Lia had never seen one like it. It was magnificent.

Emile approached a bark and pushed it into the water. He held out his hand to Lia, who took it between excitement and fear that she would soon be in the open sea. Kéo looked at the ship first with a nervous smile and helped Rose into the bark. Emile handed an oar to Kéo, who took it without enthusiasm.

When they pulled up on the dock, Emile asked Kéo to help him pull up the bark they had arrived in.

"Where are your sailors?" asked Kéo.

"No need," Emile ironically said.

"It is impossible. Given the size of this ship, it is impossible to operate it with four people," replied Kéo in shock.

"This is not a simple ship. Go to the hold. There is enough to eat and rest. Let us not dwell on the matter."

Lia, too tired to eat, went down to a cabin and slept for hours. When she woke up, it was already dark. She went to the kitchen, Kéo was preparing breakfast.

"Aren't you going to go to sleep soon?" asked Lia.

"No, I'm too anxious. Like me, you must have heard stories about people going to sea and not coming back alive! I'm not sure if it was a good idea to get on this ship." Kéo admitted while turning his back to Lia.

"I don't really believe in legends and stuff. There must be an explanation," Lia paused. "We must be far from the village by now, far from my family. I wish they were with us to get away from this world. Too bad I didn't meet Emile earlier."

"Sure, and your father would have followed you," in an amused tone.

Lia laughed out loud and they both laughed for a few moments before she got up to walk on the dock.

A little fresh air would do her good. She sat down on a ledge and gazed into the endless background. She hoped to find some peace by looking out over the ocean.

"I hope you had a good rest. We still have a few days left," interrupted Emile.

"Although I don't know anything about navigation, it seems to me that your ship sails much faster than it should. What is its secret?"

"We'll say we're not alone!" said Emile mysteriously.

"Do you have help? I thought you didn't have a sailor?"

"If I told you the truth, you wouldn't believe me. You'll find out soon enough!"

Then there was silence. Emile's eyes were fixed on the ocean. He looked serene, as if the world did not affect him. She wished she were like him. As Spirit joined her and sat down at her feet, Emile turned around, looking embarrassed.

"Thank you for trusting me. It means a lot to me" he was blushing, almost embarrassed.

Lia smiled, "I hope I wasn't wrong about you, Emile."

"If that's the case! What do you think I'm looking for?"

"Just company? Maybe you're enlisting us in some crazy quest? For money?" she said, half amused.

"Maybe so," he replied mysteriously. "I sincerely hope that one day everything will work out for you. I don't know you well, but you're not a bad person."

"I guess so. But the more time I spend with you, the harder it is to understand you. I'm usually pretty good at it, but this..."

"Maybe you like me?" said Emile with a hopeful tone.

Lia smirked and peered out at the ocean before replying,

"I have a theory. I think that the person you came looking for was me. Why did you do that? I don't know, but there are too many coincidences for it to be random. You are not someone who gives up easily. What did you go to Arrow for? You would have gone back no matter what by now."

He was silent for a few moments.

"And if that's the case, why follow me? If you are right, I did it for one purpose only and that's for money!" said Emile.

"I understand you have principles. I don't think you're the same kind of person as the mobsters. I follow my instincts and wait to see what happens to me. Father always told me to follow my instincts. He was never wrong. I hope he's right."

"Brave or foolish, I don't know how to define you yet." He smiled at her, then put his hand over hers. "I won't hurt you, I've done things in my life I'm not proud of. You're right about one thing. I don't hurt people. It doesn't matter why. But I have to tell you that in this quest, I never thought I would find someone like you. I hope that one day you will accept someone in your life, someone who is more than a friend," he respected a moment of silence. "Well, I have to get back to my business."

She watched him leave and sat waiting for hours. She had no idea how she would react if he kissed her, although she wanted to. She couldn't see herself having a love story at this time in her life, so dark and uncertain.

As the days passed Rose became sick. She stayed most of the time locked up, far from the tumult of the sea. Kéo only went out for a few moments to get some fresh air otherwise, he stayed near Rose.

Lia took advantage of the few remaining days to learn more about navigation, although the mystery of who was navigating remained unclear. For the rest of their time, Lia and Emile spent the nights talking about the stars and the days telling each other about their childhood. On this subject, Lia was more equivocal, and Emile remained vague.

In the late afternoon, they arrived near a beach surrounded by a forest. They set foot on land, waiting for Emile to take a direction. Lia left her dog on the ship, and Emile promised that they would return for him as soon as they could.

She didn't know where they were going, but she was sure she had made the right decision. The further they went, the more hopeful she became about finding her family and the more she believed she would fight for it.

11

A tragic destiny

George and his sons were locked in a cage that led them straight to the city of the *damned* in the territory of King Hilarion.

This city had a reputation for being cursed. It is said that when one entered it, it was to find death. The occupants of this city were the king's thieves, and prisoners were brought to them. Before killing them, they were tortured in the hope of obtaining useful information.

This city was ruled by the king's right-hand man, a man whose origins were unknown. He was an evil incarnate, and his name was Ciaran. He was authoritarian and ambitious, which made him feared more than respected. Even though he was not of his lineage, the king loved him more than his own sons and yet still considered him to be illegitimate since he was not of his bloodline.

People of the time considered the blood tie to be the most valuable asset, honoring a family's bloodline. George always felt that privileging a bloodline was overkill. While respecting one's origins is important, there are many things on earth that cannot be controlled. The bonds of the heart are created beyond reason. The love between two people is not based on the bond of blood and yet it is just as powerful.

George loved his wife and he will never stop loving her. The day they met was the most memorable moment of his life. She saved his soul. He still remembers the smile she gave him when she saw him for the first time.

He was already living in the village of the Molière. His father had asked him to collect taxes from each merchant and villager. Caroline was at the tavern. When she saw him enter, she smiled at him. He sat down and asked her if she wanted to keep him company, as he had not seen such a beautiful woman for a long time. She agreed and they talked for a while. She asked why he was charging people such exaggerated amounts. Their first discussion was not what he expected, and their first meeting was more like a debate, an honest confrontation of ideas.

At the time, George was an arrogant man and proud of his reputation, which was all that mattered to him. So he defended his position with aplomb and exaggeration, rather than conviction.

She left the tavern and told him that he had not yet opened his eyes to the world and that human beings should be treated with more consideration. She went on to say that our actions represent who we are, and one day, the karma that we bestow will return back to us. He chuckled as he watched her walk away. Of course, he didn't agree, but he liked the way she stood up to him, especially since he had the power to send her to the iron. Yet she did not hesitate to attack him, she was not afraid of him.

A few days later, as he was riding his horse, he came across her again. She was picking berries on the edge of the forest. He asked her about her presence. At first she ignored him. George was offended and decided not to leave until she said something. It took all day. They looked at each other in silence, waiting for the other one to give in. Suddenly they came across a wild boar, which, wanting to protect its young, charged them. They succeeded just in time to climb a tree. Laughing at this situation, they waited up there for a while, talking about their childhood.

This incongruous adventure allowed them to break the ice. Since that day, they never left each other. In the days that followed, they often met in the forest, like two lovers. She passed on her knowledge of plants and George taught her to ride a horse and to shoot a bow, which she admitted she could never do properly. She was far too fragile and sensitive to take the life of a living being.

Two months later, when he took his father's place as head of the village of the Molière, he confessed his love for her and asked her to marry him. Léonard,

George's father, having received a harsh education, refused their union, but being now the master of the place, he no longer had a say in the matter. Leonard reproached him for having changed because of this woman, and in fact, for not being strong and firm enough to rule a kingdom. It took authority to strike fear into the hearts of the people. His father felt that he was ruining what he had managed to build.

He had it all wrong. For George what they had built was the most beautiful thing in their lives. He had learned over time that the world was full of surprises, and that strength came from love, not fear. They made their kingdom a haven of peace. George wished it had lasted much longer, even though he knew a day like this would come. He hoped his children would be safe, and it didn't matter that he was the only one paying the price. He wanted so much to tell Lia that despite everything, he loved her. Maybe he hadn't been gentle enough with his children, but he wanted them to toughen up for what was about to come. Now he and his sons were at the mercy of cruel men.

"Father, what will happen to us?" asked John.

"Things you are not prepared for."

"What can we do?" said Alexander, "There must be a way out?"

"I am afraid not," said George darkly.

They fell silent, and at that moment, George knew there were things he had to tell them before it was too late, before they reached the border where they would be separated. He knew that there was still hope for his sons; his life, on the other hand, would end. Strangely, he was serene. He had lived a life filled with love. Despite his mistakes, his choices were dictated by a single goal, to see his children learn that life is a gift that should not be wasted, and that hope is always present even when it does not appear so.

"Listen to me carefully. Once we reach the borders, they will probably want to stay overnight in the first village. We won't stay in these cages, and they will move us to other prisons. If any of you manage to leave, continue without looking back."

"If that happens! I doubt it. Where will we go?" doubted Samuel.

"It will be necessary to join Chavallois Benoni. He will help you."

"I thought he didn't like us." whispered Alexander frantically. "You always said he doesn't share our views on life. Why would he help us?"

"Who can we really trust? Our king is in league with King Hilarion, and you were there when Tharsile told us. We are alone now," replied Samuel.

"Let's find our family and go somewhere!" added John angrily.

"To go where? "scoffed Alexander. 'We have no choice but to find Benoni.'

'Calm down!" spat George. "He will help us. You don't know everything. If we're both on the outs, it's because I made a decision in my life when you met Lia. He didn't accept what I did."

His sons glared at him. With each word he spoke, he saw them turn paler. He didn't know how they would react. It might change their idea of family forever. But George had to let them in on the secret before there was no hope of his family ever being together again.

When he finished, they said nothing. They looked away. Then John spoke up.

"In fact, we suspected as much. We had come across Benoni, and our meeting was most strange. He asked curious questions. In spite of this conversation nothing changes for us. We have lived our lives together, and we are a family. The rest doesn't matter. We will make sure that it stays the same. So then, this secret stays where it is for now because from where we are, there is little chance that we can solve anything!"

"You're funny. Nothing will change." replied Alexander in a low, faint hiss. "That's impossible. If we manage to escape, things will never go back to the way they were."

"No, but you can do your best to make them better," George comforted them.

"Father, you forget that we have no power and that the things that are about to begin are far above us."

"Alexander, that's where you're wrong. When you find your sister, everything will be clearer and she will need you. She'll need you to believe in us again, and especially in her."

The silence imposed itself spontaneously, and they began to penetrate the domain of King Hilarion.

A few kilometers further on, the scenery had changed radically. The forest was certainly the same, but the leaves were crimson green, and there were hardly any flowers. Nature was dying as if it understood that things were about to change.

They arrived at a barracks. The dwellings were miserable, and their occupants had a mean look. The children were busy cutting up rabbits, or practicing their archery on live targets. Everything resembled disarray and cruelty. When they arrived, they looked at them with disdain.

Suddenly a child threw a knife in the direction of George and his sons, fortunately he missed them. The wagon stopped, and a man got off his horse. It was Ciaran. George recognized him easily by the marks on his face, surrounded by a surprisingly gray head of hair. George remembered that he had not seen him fight at the Colombier, but he was not surprised that it was him who was in charge of this whole operation. It could only be someone high up. Ciaran turned to the child.

"It is forbidden to touch the prisoners!" he said sharply.

"Why?" the child whispered, holding his gaze, "since you're going to torture them," he added with a sarcastic air.

"Yes, but are you part of the king's guard?"

"No," the child replied without a hint of fear in his voice.

Ciaran gave the child a smug look, "That's what I thought," and with one swift motion he hit the child in the child in the face and nodded his consent to the men behind him. They beat him up, then one of them took a rope and strangled him with it while Ciaran looked on in satisfaction. He turned back to the other kids.

"This is what happens when you don't follow the law," he threatened them with a triumphant smile.

No one had moved. Some had watched the spectacle with greed, others with disgust. Then Ciaran walked towards his horse, as if it were a normal thing to do. Alexander spat in his face.

"To attack a child is cowardly!"

Ciaran wiped his face as he stared at him, then turned and whipped Alexander in the face.

"Next time, have more respect for the one who will torture you. With you, I'm going to get my kicks," Ciaran walked away with a furious step.

George turned to Alexander and handed him a torn cloth from his pocket.

"Here, put this on your face."

"What were you thinking? "Samuel asked.

"Even if these kids are just scoundrels, they don't deserve this! Nobody does!"

The cart set off again. The cages clashed. The landscape was as gloomy as ever.

Later that night, they arrived at an inn in a village of King Hilarion. Most of the guards went off to enjoy themselves, leaving the carriage and the prisoners out in the cold. One man whispered something to the other two who were watching them.

"Show us your hands."

George motioned to his sons to obey.

"Yes, do what Daddy says. But soon, you will regret being part of this family."

They all laughed as they chained their hands as each one was ushered out of the cage. Two more men arrived and pushed them to the back of a house.

"You'll be sleeping with the pigs tonight, but it won't change your daily routine," he said, catching a good laugh at his own joke.

The jokes they were sending each other made them happy. They took more of a mocking and sarcastic laugh. They led them to a hay shed where four men were already standing. They threw the wires inside, still hooting at their jokes. The door slammed on their heels.

A man directed George to another shed. In this room, there was only one man, and his name was the executioner. George recognized him by the x-mark on his cheek.

The men who were tortured were branded. This was not a good sign. What awaited him here would be far from pleasure.

"Ciaran said I could start having fun. You're lucky. You're the first," he laughed as he strapped him into a chair.

He started by hitting him, then after a few minutes, he grabbed a sword that was lying in the fire and enjoyed applying it to parts of his body.

His torture lasted long enough to exhaust him, but not to kill him. Ciaran had a monopoly on torture when they reached the city of the damned. They brought him back to his sons, who threw themselves at him, horrified at his condition.

"I'm fine, stop worrying!" George said pushing them away.

"Father, we are going to get out of here tonight," John whispered gleefully.

"how?"

The other prisoners looked at them as one stepped forward.

"I don't know why you are here, but you are lucky."

"Lucky to be tortured?" replied Alexander ironically.

"No to leave here!" said the man who didn't understand his ironic tone.

"What do you mean?" George stood up as best he could in front of the man.

"If you had arrived a few hours later, we would have been transported to a slave town. We've been locked up for so long that we've had time to make knives. thanks to them, we will be able to remove our chains and hopefully open this door. As for the guards, we have a chance to neutralize them, since we are more numerous."

"But once outside, it's every man for himself!" added another man.

"Given your father's condition, he would delay us too much."

Samuel was irritated at their last statement. "He's in good shape. I wouldn't worry about it. I've seen him in worse situations," he replied hoping to discourage whatever they were thinking.

They all looked at each other. On the way, they had prepared for the worst, but not for hope.

The man with the knife went to George and his sons to free them from their chains. Then he ran to the door, followed by the other men.

Cautiously, he opened the door. Outside, everyone took their positions, close to one of the guards posted in the corners. George and his sons crawled toward a group of men on their right. George headbutted one of them, though his ribs hurt. He resisted the pain, which increased with each lift of his arm.

His sons were able to prevent the other men from taking their weapons. When they were all down, George also took something to defend himself.

"Quickly, let's hurry before someone notices we're gone."

They ran through the woods. One of the men from the prison had followed them, and the others had run in the opposite direction.

Unfortunately for them, they were headed for the village and would surely find worse than death.

Having paid attention to the route, George could manage to find the direction to return to their borders.

They ran, pausing a few times without uttering a word, listening for the slightest sound. They still needed a few hours to reach the border.

As they were about to enter King Theodore's domain, they heard horses.

"My sons, listen to me carefully. I will hold them off as long as I can. Continue south. It should only be a few more miles to our house. Once there, you should be able to find your way back."

"We won't leave without you!" Alexander was determined to protect his life.

"We don't have time to talk. I need you alive. Get out of here!" George he said sharply.

"I will stay with your father. I have no one else waiting for me," replied an old man.

George glared at them. John was the first to give the impetus to leave, and push his brothers. The last thing he saw of them was their eyes glowing in the darkness as they made their way into the forest.

"Thank you, what is your name? I like to know the name of an ally."

"Robert," raising his hand.

"I'm George," shaking his hand friendly.

A group of men, led by Ciaran, came rushing toward them. When George saw them firing arrows in his direction, he jumped in time to dodge them. One of the arrows hit a guard behind him. George managed to hit two more guards before Ciaran ran straight at him. Three more men attacked George while the other four went after his sons.

Robert was already in trouble with a man, perhaps even the first time he had fought.

George killed two guards. Ciaran hit him in the shoulder. He lost his balance but managed to hit him back. Their joust lasted a while.

Exhausted by the pain, George stumbled. This allowed Ciaran to hit him in the head and knock him down.

At that moment, he saw his companion fall after being shot in the chest. He heard Ciaran yell at the other two to drag him to his cage and lock him in.

George smiled, because his sons were gone. Even though his fate was grim, they were not with him to see it. He would have liked to be there in the next few months, and he would have liked to protect them again so that they would not have to go through terrible trials alone.

He hoped now that Caroline had her children with her, that she would bring them to Mount Celeste safe and sound.

12

The leak

John and his brothers ran for a few days before the mounted guards were on their heels. They barely rested, just what their bodies needed. Their father gave them time, probably not enough, but just what they needed. They had just entered King Theodore's land when they saw a narrow corridor running into the earth, and they didn't hesitate to take it.

They made their way through the stones of the ancient ruins that did not allow horses to venture. The ancient walls, which nature had resumed its natural course amongst, were a mystery to the people. Since it had been there for so long no one knew what ancient civilization they originally belonged to. Only one clue made people think that they must have been small, because hardly a man could enter this long open corridor.

Even if the corridor was not too long, it gave the brothers extra time. The horsemen had to make a bigger detour to catch up with them since, this ancient rune was extraordinarily surrounded by deep water over a long distance.

The boys were already ahead of the game from the hallway exit, but the horseman wasn't planning on letting up anytime soon. They were tough men, trained to overcome pain. They didn't have to wait long to hear an arrow whistle toward them. They decided to face their attackers. Running around like this was useless. They were armed only with a few swords, which they had picked up. All they had to do was wait.

Suddenly a man came up with his bow and shot at them. They dodged easily. Alexander climbed the tree in front of him with ease and jumped from branch to branch to land on the captor. He escaped another arrow and gave him a blow. The man fell, but got up quickly and grabbed his sword, ready to fight Alexander.

Three more men arrived to surround John and Samuel. John began to fight. The men were very good with swords. The brothers struggled to keep up. Alexander joined them after successfully shooting the man with the bow. One of the men hit Samuel in the shoulder and he screamed in pain. Alexander and John managed to take them out one by one while their brother lay on the ground.

John crouched down beside him.

"Samuel, can you hear me? This is not the time to play. Wake up! We're not there yet!"

"We have to move! We don't know if others are still on our tail. We will carry him each in turn," shouted John to Alexander.

"He won't last long. He needs to be treated."

"Can you do it? I can't, so in the meantime, we have to keep going," said John, snarling at him.

John began to carry him. Samuel was heavy. The road ahead was difficult. He had to find help as soon as possible. It was getting cold. They were not going to be able to hold out.

"Alex, take the lead. See if we can't find some help. I keep moving down the path. It won't hold."

Alexander dashed forward, while John stumbled heavily on the ground. Between fatigue and the weight of his brother, it was a step too far. He got back up to Samuel, hoping he hadn't hurt him more.

Then suddenly, he heard someone approaching. Footsteps were coming towards him. It could have been Alexander as well as other guards, so he chose to be cautious and drew his sword.

"It's only me. I found a farmer. He is coming with his wife and daughter. They can help us. I only told them that bandits attacked us."

"All right, come help me lift him, we already lost almost a day!"

An elderly man arrived and helped them. They carried their brother in silence. The settlement was modest, but luckily challenging to reach. You would have had to know the area to spot it.

The man put Samuel in a room and his wife asked them to leave. She and her daughter were going to treat him. They had been lucky; the farmer's wife had once worked as a nurse.

"It's a good thing we're still here, we were supposed to be on our way to Arrow by now, but we've fallen behind. Here, drink this. It's a little wine I make myself," said the farmer.

"Thank you, for the wine, but mostly for your help," replied John.

"You'll thank me when your man is on his feet."

The farmer walked to the door and before leaving, said.

"I apologize but I have to go unsaddle the horses. Night is already here!"

Then he left. John and Alexander were exhausted. They didn't know when they would be able to get back on the road, but they had to.

"Maybe one of us should go to Goose Castle? We're wasting time," said Alexander.

"No, we stay together! It's too dangerous to separate now. It can wait."

John didn't answer anymore; he knew his brother was right, but he also knew that the little hope of helping their father was being consumed as time passed on that farm. He couldn't resign himself to losing him forever. Their family was separated, and he had no power over it. He had to find solutions, to act as soon as possible. John would not stand by and do nothing. He would defend his family's honor till his last breath.

After a few hours, the man returned, at the same time as his wife in the kitchen. John and Alexander stood up, as one, and waited for her to speak.

"Your brother will be fine, he's resting for now, but he won't be able to get back on the road right away."

"When?" asked John.

"A week," she said, taking a glass of water.

"We can't wait that long! What about tomorrow?" John said desperately.

Cautiously she informed them that the wound could open again if they moved him too much. They were desperate, yet they had to leave.

Suddenly the farmer's daughter entered the kitchen. She was tall, rather thin, with beautiful black hair, and blue eyes. She was wiping her hands of their brother's blood when she spoke in a serene tone.

"I think I can help you. In two days, I'm going to drive some cattle south. I'm leaving in a wagon, so I can drop you off wherever you want."

"Thank you for your kindness. We gladly accept," said Alexander.

"We are heading south, too," added John with mistrust.

"I'm going a little further. It will take us a week or more. You're pretty brave to have wanted to walk the road," she smiled at them, then returned to the room.

Sure, she was beautiful and even bewitching, but John was wary of her. Something was wrong. He decided not to tell her their true destination.

"Excuse me, I am losing my manners. My name is Ivan and my wife is Celeste. As for our daughter, her name is Honoré."

"It's a pleasure. We call ourselves the brotherhood. Does your daughter help you in the fields?" asked Alexander.

"Oh no, she left at a very young age, to work as a servant for the king. We don't know more. She is very quiet, and even more enigmatic since she is working there. What do you want? Life changes each of us."

The moment Ivan mentioned the king, John's heart almost stopped. He wasn't really sure anymore if this trip in the presence of the young woman was a good idea.

"Alexander, let's get some fresh air. Excuse us. We'd like to take our minds off things."

"Yes, of course! Do so, my wife prepares a good dinner. She is an excellent cook, you will see."

They got up and left their hosts' home. Once outside, they moved far enough away to be within earshot.

"Did you hear what I heard? We can't risk going with her," said John.

"What? Of course, it does. It doesn't mean she's a spy. It's just coincidence, and we don't have much choice but, to tell the truth."

"I am not sure. We never know!"

"Look, she's alone, and she's a servant. We have nothing to worry about. What else do you want to do? Wait longer?" Alexander's eyebrows furrowed together as he spoke.

"No, of course not. You're right. We have no choice."

They went back inside, where dinner was waiting for them. They were hungry. They hadn't eaten in so long. After dinner, they slept on the floor. Ivan apologized for this rudimentary comfort, but John and Alexander were so tired that anything would do.

13

A future destiny

*I*t was now six days since John and his brothers had been on their way to Goose Castle with Honoré.

It was going to be a long road. Samuel was sleeping less and could now speak, although he was still very weak. So they had to take turns watching over him at the back of the cart.

Honoré seemed to like Samuel and vice versa. Together they talked a lot, which began to worry John. He decided to have a word with his brother, while Honoré stood by the horse pushing the cart

"Hey Samuel, what are you talking about with this girl?"

"What? Are you jealous that she is interested in me?" Samuel replied as a smirk tugged at his lips.

"Not at all! What are you talking about! I'm just wondering if she's trying to seduce you to trick us," he replied stiffly.

Samuel tries to stand up, wedged between a straw mattress and a cushion, but the posture revives the pain. As soon as Samuel moaned, Honoré stopped the cart and turned abruptly. She looked at him worriedly, her hand on the horse's side, then without an ounce of hesitation, she ran in his direction.

"Stop bothering your brother. He needs to rest. Come on!"

"I have to talk to him!" anger and nerves shook John's voice. "You will do it later. You will have time then. We still have a few days left," she said turning her back on him.

John left his brother and walked back to Alexander, disappointed that he could not finish the discussion.

"Alexander, I think it will soon be time to run away from our savior," he mentioned while nervously scratching his head.

"What do you mean by that?" Alexander stopped for a second and looked at him.

"In two days, we will be very close to Goose of Castle. I know a passage that can only be taken on foot. It will be safer and it would be wise to part with Honoré as soon as possible. Did you manage to talk to our brother in private, because I didn't?"

"I didn't get to talk to him. But I don't see it as a threat. I mostly think they're infatuated," John said amused.

"Maybe, but either way, we'll part in two days."

"Okay. Plus, he looks pretty good now," John said looking in Samuel direction.

***

A few days had passed, and the sun was weighing on the mount and on the group. They decided to stop in the shade of a tree. Only a few birds interrupted the abrupt silence. John waited impatiently for this moment to speak with his brother.

"You again! Decidedly you are stubborn!!" reproached Honoré in a not very friendly tone.

"You have no idea, my dear," Samuel sneered.

They looked at each other and smiled. He couldn't explain it, but John didn't like the closeness at all. He felt like they had just lost his brother.

"In fact, I want to talk to both of you. Alexander and I have decided..." Samuel stopped him from talking.

"Since when do you decide for me? Am I not the eldest?" imposing himself with pride before Honoré.

"What? Someone has to make decisions while you're cooing!" John spat out.

"So that's it!" crossing his arms angrily.

"Come on, that's enough!" Before continuing, he looked at them, "we leave on our side. Thank you, Honoré for your welcome and your help, but it is now time for us to continue our way. Some family business awaits us," John glanced at his brother, in case he had forgotten the urgency of the situation.

"What?" Samuel was nearly screaming. "And since when do you speak for me?"

"To decide together, it would have been necessary that we manage to speak to you, alone," Alexander cut him off.

"Easy to say, I'm the one who's hurt. Let's stop this childishness and get to the facts. I don't follow you."

"What?" exclaimed John and Alexander in unison.

"The situation will remain as it is for me. Honoré, on the other hand, needs my help, she has problems and this is a situation that I can remedy."

"Have you forgotten even your sisters?" said John, shocked by the turnaround.

"How dare you? Of course not, but from there to abandon our convictions. I'm sorry, but my choice is made, yours too. I won't keep you. We will meet again, I will join you," he tried to speak with a calm voice.

Alexander started to approach him to retort, but John stopped him. Then they stayed to look at him leaving, in the cart, at the sides of Honoré, victorious, who until then had remained a silent spectator.

"Why did you let him go like that?" asked Alexander.

"Have you forgotten his stubborn and impetuous character? Anyway, we are running out of time. No need to waste any more of it chatting. He has made his decision. I only hope that this Honoré is trustworthy."

Then, they moved away in turn, to continue their journey.

***

The days of walking had exhausted them, but they were finally approaching the village of Gleenay, which they had to bypass to reach their destination.

John's heart ached. He hoped to find help and answers. He didn't know where their family was or if they were suffering at this very moment. But they needed them, and even more so at this moment, they were counting on them.

Alexander ran forward.

"Look at the path. Here we are. At least we have a chance not to run into any guards."

They continued in silence, both worried about being helpless.

They approached the house. The path led to the barns.

They stayed for a while, observing the surroundings. They did not want to meet anyone, not even a servant. They could not trust anyone.

After a few moments, they saw Julienne Chavallois. John whistled to get her attention. He didn't know if she had spotted them. At the same time, a servant joined her, and they hid in the back of the barn. They were silent, holding their breath for a few moments, then someone approached.

A head appeared. It was Julienne.

"We were waiting for you. Come quickly. I have sent our servants further away. Let's hurry!" she muttered frantically.

They swiftly followed her. She led them to the basement, where she locked them in. John wondered if it was a trap.

A few hours later, she returned with an apology.

"I'm sorry, we had to send away several servants who are suspected of being unfaithful. My husband is waiting for you in his office. Follow me."

They followed her in silence, anxious about what they might learn. Benoni sat at his desk.

He was an elegant man, always dressed in an officer's uniform that made his build even more imposing. His face, although friendly, had a fierce look due to his long beard. When he saw them, he stood up.

"I am sorry for you and your family. Come on in, have a seat. We have some things to talk about."

"Father advised us to come to you. He said you could help us," said John as he sat down. "Father couldn't get away, but he gave us a chance. He's in a town called *Damned*, and we have to do something."

"Listen to me carefully," Benoni answered calmly. "Unfortunately, there is nothing I can do for your father. It would take an army, and even if we managed to gather one, it would already be too late for him."

"Too late?" repeated Alexander between fright and disappointment. "He said you were going to help us..."

"Yes, and he's right. You, your family, your secret."

"Yes, we know," said John sadly.

Alexander remained silent. The shock of their father's sealed fate had hit him, stunned. John too, but he had to stay strong. His sisters had to be found.

"Well, I do know where your sisters, Monica and Ayana, are. I didn't wait for you to send one of my best knights."

"Only one?" Alexander questioned dryly.

"King Hilarion's territory is austere, spies in every corner. Surprisingly, a single man has a better chance of going unnoticed than an armed group," he paused before continuing. "The city in question is known for selling slaves. I don't want to start a war that we can't win. The man I sent is clever. I trust him."

John put his hand on his brother's shoulder, wanting to retort.

"Thank you for your help. We appreciate it, and we are exhausted. Please excuse us."

"No need to apologize, boys. You've been through the worst."

"It's only just begun, I think," confided Alexander, on the verge of tears.

"As you know, our king Theodore has allied himself with our worst enemy, King Hilarion, so it's time to go on the offensive."

He stood up and took a few steps, before continuing.

"Indeed, I can help you. I have suspected for some time that he was doing something wrong. I have men, warriors ready to fight for me, but also for you. But there are not enough of us for the war that is brewing. I hope I can find support from King Leon. Tomorrow, my advisor and I will leave for Arrow. In the meantime, I ask you to stay here and protect my domain. Normally there is nothing to fear, but it is best to remain cautious. Take the opportunity to meet our allies, talk to them, they need to trust us."

"You can count on us," said John.

"Your brother, Samuel, what happened to him?"

"He is doing well. At least he was the last time we saw him. He will join us later."

"Good, because we will have a better chance of training valiant soldiers with him. If you'll excuse me, it's time for me to prepare for my trip. Make yourself at home. We'll show you to your rooms."

"Wait, please, my mother, Thomas, Georgina and Lia, do you know where they are?" he stood up quickly.

"I am afraid, I don't. I only know that your mother managed to escape, Lia too, but they are separated. May protection be with them and on all of us."

With that, he left the room. They were too tired to look for more information, so they decided to go to their room. They had been left some food, but John was exhausted and fell asleep immediately after lying down in his bed.

The next morning he woke up early, unable to sleep. He was devastated by the fate of their father, and the thought of it was in his mind, and he couldn't get it out of his head.

He joined his brother in the kitchen.

"I hope you slept better than I did," John asked.

"Not really," he replied, still mourning.

"Benoni left this morning. He left us with a list of people to rely on, and another with those who need more persuasion."

"Let's start now. The sooner the better. I can't stand not doing anything."

John agreed. They left for the office, and on the way, they passed Julienne, looking glum and tired.

"Julienne, thanks again for what you do and for your hospitality. You look very pale!"

"Excuse me. I am constantly worried whenever my husband is away."

"I understand, but your husband is resourceful. He will come back. If there is anything you need, don't hesitate to come to us."

John and Alexander greeted her and took their leave. As they reached the office, Alexander broke out of the silence.

"Poor Julienne, I feel guilty."

"He would have left whether we were here or not," he said swiftly. "Where do we start?"

"Let's meet the ones who are ready to fight first, and then tomorrow, we'll go to the others," suggested Alexander.

At the end of the morning, they left for the agreed meeting point in the woods, by Benoni.

About fifty men were waiting for them, and John began to address everyone.

"Benoni told us about his plan and your courage. I thank you for your commitment to this cause. The battle has not begun and we may be few in number but we will fight for peace and for the safety of our families. Until Benoni returns, in the immediate future, we will train and try to gather as many volunteers as possible. Do any of you know a place that is hidden and safe enough?"

For a few moments no one spoke, then a short, thin man stepped forward.

"I know one, Sir. I spent my whole childhood there, hidden from my violent father. It's a cave big enough for us to take refuge in."

"That will fit, thank you! What is your name?"

"Telo, sir."

"Right. Telo, let's go, shall we? As for the others, we'll meet in two days at this place. Telo will take you there."

They answered with a nod, and the men dispersed.

Telo led John and Alexander through the woods. It was a little over an hour's walk, but the cave was perfect, deep, quite remote, and out of sight.

The next morning, John and Alexander visited a lone trader several miles away. There they were to meet a group of men, craftsmen or carpenters. They were honest people, working hard to keep their families alive, and wanted to fight for a better life for their own. They were insecure and some had never even held a gun.

Alexander was rather doubtful, because they were not warriors at all, so he spoke to his brother. John supported the plan, and for that, he added.

"I disagree, Alexander. The greatest warriors were craftsmen, their will based on a hope that their lives would change. No matter what they become."

"You're talking about a handful of men who stood out, but the rest died in battle."

"Maybe, but hope is sometimes the best motivation, I trust. Tell yourself that anyway, we have no choice. And we will train them!"

Alexander nodded his head in agreement, and then they entered the merchant's home.

Most of the men were young, but all of them were terrified, looking around as if some evil being was haunting the place. John walked over to them and spoke.

"Thank you for coming in such numbers. I know what it's like to be terrified, as you are. I have to tell you something. When I was six years old, my father forced me to handle a bow. We went hunting. At the time, the thought of killing anyone scared me. But I had to be strong like all the men in the family. During the hunt, there was this deer. It was not dead, although I hit it badly. He asked me to finish it off and take out its heart. It is our custom for the first hunt of a man, that the one who kills, tears out his heart. I succeeded and like me, you will succeed. For different reasons, but everyone will find the courage. If you are ready, meet at the edge of the woods, we can start training now. We will not force anyone, but know that if you fight, it is to give hope to our children and grandchildren. Can you bear to live in fear? My father made us know peace, taste the hope of happiness and know that it exists. We must rise up and take control of our lives and the lives of our loved ones."

"Excuse me Sir, but for you it will be easy. We could lose everything."

"We have nothing left. They took everything away from us. My family is scattered. Some may be dead. I am fighting for their hope, for the hope of seeing them again, of finding a serene life! If you are in, follow me!"

Then Alexander followed John outside, and to their surprise, everyone followed. They arrived at the cave where Telo was waiting. They had gathered a whole bunch of weapons.

"My friends, at first, we will fight with wooden weapons. Then for those who are more skilled, we will start training with real weapons. Let's go!"

They had succeeded in their first mission, that of gathering people and giving them the motivation to join their group. Now they just had to hope that events would unfold as planned. Time was short.

14

The ambush

A month and a half passed, and the boys had no news of Benoni or their brother Samuel. Julienne was frightened by the fate that lay ahead and she felt terribly alone.

Telo came by every morning to bring good news. Every day, allies joined the troops, and the men who trained became real warriors day after day.

The army was slowly taking shape, and with it, hope was emerging.

It was late evening, and John and Alexander were in Benoni's office when a heavyset man stormed in.

"You must be the Leusire family?"

"Yes, that's us," said John. "Who are you?"

"I am Benoni's advisor, Marc."

At Benoni's name, John and Alexander immediately stood up.

"Is he okay?" asked Alexander.

"Yes, but before I speak could I have a good drink. I am thirsty. I came as fast as I could."

John waved to Alexander, who immediately moved to the back of the room, to the sideboard that housed the bottles of wine.

As with their father's home, there was always plenty of room for people to drop in unannounced, to celebrate, or to comfort each other in the office.

He drank in one gulp, and while pouring himself a second glass, he began his story.

"He's fine, for now. He's in a meeting with the governor, who is managing the situation. He has the power to grant the audience with the king or not. We suspect he is trying to waste time. He is not always honest, and he plays on all fronts. Benoni made an excuse to come and warn you to be on your guard and take care of his wife in case things go wrong. Don't trust anyone. Tomorrow I'll go back and try to find a king's guard, hoping to get an audience, otherwise, we're lost."

"Did you find out what the governor is up to?" asked Alexander.

"We just know, that he is in contact with a man from the City of the Damned."

At the name of the place, John and Alexander remained silent, and bowed their heads.

"I'm sorry to bring back bad memories. I, too, would like to forget this name and especially this place, or rather this abyss!"

John approached, "Tell me more about this place,."

"Why?" replied Alexander.

"I need to know. I can't stop thinking about father and maybe learning a little more about this city would help me move on."

"Fine kid, if you want. Although it doesn't seem like a good idea," he poured himself another glass of wine and sank into the chair.

"I was about your younger brother's age when it all started. My father was convicted of treason by one of our neighbors. At the time, we were living near the border of King Theodore. We were taken prisoner. Now I understand better why we were brought there. At that time, Theodore was just beginning negotiations with King Hilarion for power," he paused. "This city was already chilling just by looking at it from afar. It looked like the abyss of evil. King Hilarion built this city in a mountain of rock. The first time King Hilarion saw this hill, it is said that he was struck by a deity who whispered to him to build his future here. Through this city, he expected to learn the secrets of the people that would allow him to gain power. For this, he had to be even crueler than he already was. The construction was quickly completed. He demanded to build a gigantic hollow in the rock and build a castle at the top, on the periphery of the crater. The people who lived there were the poorest in his kingdom. The dwellings that were built in the rock, were as gloomy as the place. To work there, one had to want to earn a living. The heat and humidity were unbearable, although for more than half the day there was little sunlight. Moreover, life was miserable, and the village was dirty and dangerous. The people had become villains. Although the kingdom of Hilarion was not much brighter, there was a constant fear in this village that was worse than in the other cities. Poverty had generated violence and self-centeredness. The children were hateful. When I arrived in the village, the children looked at me while playing with a knife. I must have been their age and they were envious. I was terrified. My parents and I were taken to a room in the castle. There, we were left to rot for more than a week without anything, not even a light, in complete darkness. Then, several times, they took my mother away. I never knew what happened to her, although today with my adult eyes, I can guess what happened to her. One day, as I fell asleep in her arms, I opened my eyes and tried to wake her up. That's when I realized that she would sleep forever. At that very moment, I was so sad that I wanted to die. I thought life was so cruel and unfair. When we were taken to a room filled with instruments of torture, I thought that my time had come too. Nothing was washed, dry or fresh. Blood was embedded everywhere. Bodies lay in the corners while others were still on tables. A man slapped me with a glove filled with nails. Yes, the marks you see on this face are not war scars but hate scars. For hours they tortured my father by forcing me to watch. He died very quickly from his wounds, and mental exhaustion. Since my mother's death, he was no longer himself. I thought it was my turn, so they grabbed me and threw me on a cart. Days later, I was at King Theodore's house. I thought he had saved my life. I devoted years of service to him before I found Benoni who saved what little soul I had left," he finished the bottle without bothering to pour the bottom into his glass. The memories were painful. "Well, I'm going to go rest. See you when I wake up."

John and Alexander rose to greet him, and as he walked through the door, John asked him one last question.

"Why did the king save you?"

"If you have the answer one day, kid, you tell me! I keep asking myself. Why me and not my parents?"

When he disappeared from their vision, they fell back into the chair. Both pensive, John poured himself a drink.

"We have to win this war so that we never hear this kind of story again. No more unnecessary loss of loved ones. Tomorrow we must continue training. It is our only hope."

John left his brother alone with the rest of the bottle. This story hadn't really helped them find the inner peace they were hoping for.

John had asked this question in order to find a real reason to fight, and he hoped he had not triggered the opposite.

The next day, they were training in the den when suddenly someone approached. They immediately raised their weapons.

"Sir, I am a soldier of Goose Castle. An attack is coming. One of my servants has heard that they plan to arrest everyone on the estate."

"For what reason?" asked Alexander.

"They are considered allies of your father. The king has all your friends arrested, sir."

They looked at each other and without a word, they ran as fast as they could. John stopped at the entrance to the passageway that led to the barns and looked back at Telo.

"Bring back as many men as you can, those who know how to fight. The war has just begun!" He looked at the others. "As for you, go home and barricade yourselves!"

John and his brother first ran to the house to get everyone out.

From upstairs, John saw a group of men enter the courtyard. It was too late. Alexander was coming in with weapons, Julienne and Benoni behind him.

"Ma'am, we'll get you out of here, I promise," John reassured her.

They were going to fight to the end. John hoped to hold them off as long as possible, so that reinforcements had time to arrive.

15

A desperate girl

"Samuel would you be hungry? We still have enough rabbit left. I could cook it," Honoré smiled sweetly while asking him.

"Of course, I'm starving and a good cook like you are, I'm enjoying it in advance!" he looked at her returning the sweet gesture.

His brothers did not understand him, but this was the first time Samuel really understood the meaning of love. He now understood what Lia meant.

At this thought, he lost his smile. He was torn between helping Honoré and rescuing his family. But surely it was possible to do both?

It was decided, he would come back in time. Honoré snapped him out of his thoughts, handing him a plate.

"What are you thinking about, my love?"

"I can't stop thinking about what my brothers told me. I think they are right. I am straying from my duties," he responded, looking down in sadness.

"I don't know exactly what's going on, but didn't you tell me that there's not much you can do about it right now?"

She looked at him, scared, as if he was going to abandon her. He took her hand.

"I stay! I chose to, and I always keep my promises. Beating and raping a woman is shameful, and I promise to give you justice," he said squeezing her hands tighter.

"So, in the meantime rest. If you want to avenge me you will need all your strength."

Samuel smiled at her, then finished his meal and opted for a good night's sleep. Within a week, he would be in better shape and they would arrive in Honoré's village.

***

As they reached their goal, to Samuel's astonishment, Honoré chose to go around the village and into the forest.

At his surprised look, she reassured Samuel.

"Just as a precaution!"

Now that he could walk with ease, he had regained most of his strength.

He was standing in front of her, when he heard this strange noise, which sounded like a warning. People were banging pieces of wood against metal.

Samuel looked back at Honoré, and he suddenly had a bad feeling. She was looking at the ground while murmuring, "sorry."

Suddenly, some armed men rushed towards him. He managed to fend them off. But one of them hit his weakened shoulder, and he fell to his knees. They took advantage of this moment to hold him firmly.

A short man smiled mockingly at her. He had lost a lot of teeth and was robust with long hair.

"Good, good, good Honoré," said the man with a strange curl to his lips. "But where are the others?" he asked firmly.

"They left towards the east," she said with fear smeared on her face.

She did not look at Samuel. She had betrayed him and for her, he had betrayed his brothers.

"I won't say anything, torture me if you like, but I'll keep quiet!" howled Samuel.

"Oh, man, you are of no use to me since dad has told us enough," and then he started to giggle.

Samuel turned pale, before yelling at him.

"No, he would never confess things, even under torture. He is a strong man!"

"Apparently not!" he said, laughing rudely. He brought his face close to him, "he bent like all the others, and even, I must say, quite quickly. You should have seen him, after being beating with a stick and severing one of his fingers, how can I put it, it was really exciting to see. Every man knows when he has a stronger man in front of him. And that's why he turned into a nice doggie, haha haha haha…"

Samuel wanted to retort, but they hit him with a stick, and suddenly everything went black.

Samuel woke up with a severe headache. To his surprise, he was locked in what looked like a basement, unchained. He remained alone and distressed in the darkness of the cell.

***

Two days later, he still saw no one. The lock creaked, and someone entered with a candle. Tiredness did not allow him to get up and the candlelight did not allow him to see clearly.

"I'm sorry," said a voice he could recognize. Honoré's voice, made him fume. He did not answer her. she continued to talk, "I've come to bring you food."

"Is this your idea?" asked Samuel furiously.

"Of course not! In fact, they want to feed you to better torture you, sorry…" Samuel interrupted her.

"No, to betray me?" he shouted.

"I am a martyr too. Everything I told you is true. They torture me every day. I do it for my daughter, whom they hold prisoner and…"

"Go away. I don't want to see you anymore. You disgust me," he said, turning his head not to see her.

He heard her leave, sobbing, without deigning to look at her.

Mostly he was angry with himself. He had failed in his duties. Father had counted on him and he had betrayed him, not to mention the rest of his family. He was the eldest, and in the end, he had been the least responsible. He was devastated. He was going to die, like his father. And he was going to die a coward.

He did not bother to eat and laid down on the cold ground. Bruised and alone, he accepted his fate as deserving.

16

The real reason

After several days of torture and exhaustion, Samuel finally saw the light of day. He was going to be moved to another place. He didn't know where, but he knew that he was surely running towards his end.

Honoré had come to his bedside from time to time to sponge up his blood. The first few times she tried to talk to him, but he wouldn't say a word back, so she finally gave up. She came to nurse him, which was a sign of a bad omen.

The men who were torturing him, were also trying to keep him alive, and might have done much worse to him than they are now.

Samuel was handcuffed and pushed onto a cart. The guards and servants rushed to leave, in their haste, they forgot many things, but no one seemed to care.

He saw Honoré holding a child in her arms. Men snatched the child from her. Honoré struggled. One man hit her, and she collapsed unmoving. Tied up, Samuel watched the whole scene from a distance, powerless. He saw her body shudder with sobs.

Suddenly, some men began to hit her, so hard that she lost consciousness. Samuel looked on, sickened by the violence.

He immediately understood Honoré, the one he loved, this woman protecting her child with bravery in the face of opposing barbarism. He understood then that he had been hard on her. She was defending her offspring that she loved so much. She was doing what he should have done, protecting his family.

He was hurt, because he loved her and she had betrayed him. Whether she loved him or not was not the point, her fight was more important than a man's love.

He gradually regained courage. He wanted to help her. He saw Honoré's child in the arms of a woman who must have been her nanny.

During the whole trip, Samuel observed her in her every move.

When they stopped, he saw her enter a building and to his surprise he was directed in the same direction. He heard the cries of the child in the next room.

He was made to sit in a chair, and two strong men surrounded him.

The little man nonchalantly entered the room. Samuel had not seen him since their first meeting, although he suspected he was behind all his torture.

The little man looked at him and smiled before addressing him.

"Well, let's get serious," he said with a hideous grin.

He walked around Samuel, watching him carefully, and stopped in front of a table full of instruments of torture. He picked up a pair of pliers and licked them before approaching him again.

"Well, do you know that Lia, is not really your sister?" the little man lost his smile when Samuel laughed.

"You think to destabilize me, to weaken me mentally," said Samuel with pride. He challenged him with his eyes and grinned victoriously, showing him that he would fail. "Our family secrets are no more. You are wasting your time."

"Um … actually, I don't think so. Your father is dead. Two of your sisters are prisoners and will go through hell. Your brothers are dead."

At these words, Samuel's heart tightened. It couldn't be true. He thought then, that everything was his fault. Although no tears came out, the shock of this allegation petrified him.

"Ahah, you see, you can still be surprised. Your sister Lia has abandoned you. She's gone to start a new life. She's already forgotten you. You are alone now!"

"It's all lies, lies!" he shouted like a madman.

The boy nodded his head in the direction of his men. The executioners hit him first in the face and then in the abdomen.

"Well, calmed down? Let's continue. As for your mother, she took the last two of your siblings and abandoned you too. Because you see, she keeps a well-hidden secret. She is not Lia's mother. Lia is only your cousin! This secret, you are paying for it now. It is this secret that destroyed your family, that made your father die. Lia's family is cursed. Oh what? Didn't you know that you had an aunt on your mother's side who died a long time ago? You don't know everything. This secret, my master wants it, he wants Lia!"

Then, possessed by rage, the little man went up to Samuel and cut off his finger. He screamed in pain and the lack of understanding of what was really happening in his family made him lose consciousness.

He was immersed in a nightmare and a dream at the same time. He found himself in his garden at the Colombier. Thomas and Georgina were playing ball, Spirit at their side. His mother Caroline and his sisters Ayana and Monica were having tea, while his other brothers, Lia and his father, were practicing their swordsmanship.

He knew it was all a dream because their father would never have accepted it. They all laughed together. Samuel approached and Lia came to him, took his hand and led him to them.

Suddenly, clouds covered the sun. He looked back at his sisters, they were lying dead. His mother, Thomas and Georgina had disappeared. He discovered Lia's bloody hand, she had just killed their father. She was running towards him, screaming. Suddenly, Spirit jumped on him.

He woke up in a sweat, when a soft female voice whispered to him.

"Calm down, it's only a nightmare," Honoré appeared.

"I'm not sure who my family is anymore. There are still too many secrets," he said with deep regret.

"The past is what has been, not what will be. You build your future on what your life has been, by getting better. Have hope."

"Hope?" he almost laughed.

He was still in the same dark room, since his last tête-à-tête with the little man. Releasing him from his bonds, Honoré confided to him.

"The men guarding you are going to sleep for a long time. Everyone has left, I don't know where they are or when they will return. So hurry up!"

He took her arm.

"What about you? Do you know that you will pay with your life?" he said worried.

"My own life is nothing. And it's also a way of apologizing. I sincerely regret having betrayed you."

He stood up, the pain in his hand was unbearable, but Honoré gave him courage. He walked over to the torture table, grabbed a knife and headed for the door.

"What are you doing?" asked Honoré.

"If I go out, you go out!" he said with a determined look.

"I will not leave without my daughter, and if I stay they will not kill her."

"I know, let's go get her," he pushed her to follow him.

"I don't know where she is," her voice was trembling with anxiety.

"I think I know where to find her."

She also took a knife and followed him. He stopped at the door of the next room where the baby's cries were coming from. He could hear footsteps.

He signaled to Honoré to hide. He knocked on the door and stepped aside. The nurse opened the door, at which point he hit her in the head. Honoré ran into the room, the woman tried to get up, but Samuel gave her another blow, then another. He poured out all his anger on her. She may have been innocent, but at that moment, he didn't care about anything but getting Honoré to safety.

She took his arm to stop him and waved to go ahead. On his way out, he wanted to head for the forest.

But Honoré went against the grain. She had prepared her escape. She got on a cart, and Samuel took the reins of the horses and galloped them as fast as he could.

They had traveled many miles when Samuel decided that they were far enough away to stop the carriage in a quiet place.

"We shouldn't stop," Honoré said in fear.

"We won't last long enough as it is, let alone your baby. Then we need a plan. We can't go forward without a goal."

"Can we join your brothers at Goose Castle?"

"I am afraid not," pinching his lips. "By now, there can't be much left," he continued sadly.

Honoré squeezed his arm, as a sign of compassion.

"I'm sorry. This is all my fault."

"You don't have to apologize, I do. I was hard on you when you were just trying to save the people you love, just like me."

"It's forgotten," a ghost of a smile crossed her face. "Where are we going?"

"I don't know. Towards the sea, it is one of the least guarded places. The journey will be long, but this way we will have a chance to lose our attackers."

They didn't say a word for the rest of the day and fell asleep in each other's arms.

17

A new future

More than a month had passed. Samuel, Honoré and her child had settled in a fishing village.

They had taken refuge in the home of an old lady to whom Honoré lent a hand to maintain the house and Samuel went fishing in exchange for a roof over his head.

Sure, it wasn't very glorious, but at least they were safe.

It was late, Samuel was standing on the porch, meditating as he did every evening at sunset. He wanted to find his brothers, he was still in a hope that the little man lied, but that would mean putting Honoré in danger. As soon as they found a safe place, he would leave to join the fight. Guilt gnawed at him a little more every day.

Gently, two arms embraced him.

"Don't be so pensive my love! I promise you that one day we can be happy and have a home."

He took her hand and kissed it, then lifted her to his lap.

"I am happy with you," he brought her in closer.

"So what's eating at you?"

"My duties!" he said with an half broken heart.

"I may be selfish but your duty is to us. I don't want to lose you. Their war, your war, is far too dangerous," Honoré said while holding back tears.

"If I don't get involved, we'll never be safe, always looking over our shoulders, hiding. Is that what you want for your child and our future children?"

"Of course not, but what other solution do we have?" she asked and breathing very fast.

"Fighting for our freedom, for your daughter's freedom. Even if I have to give my life, I will be happier."

She took his face and kissed it, then looked him straight in the eye.

"Not at this price. I love you so much. Let's stop talking about it, shall we? Let's go home. I'm cold, come and sleep!"

"I'll be there in a minute," he said before kissing her on the cheek.

She got up and went inside. He looked up at the stars one last time and wondered if somewhere a member of his family was watching them tonight, too. He began to make a wish to see them again one day, and to receive their forgiveness. He returned home and spent a night of passion in the arms of the woman he loved.

***

Two weeks later, as he was standing on the dock ready to embark, the old lady came to meet him.

"I wanted to thank you for the company you keep."

"Please, no," he interrupted her, "we owe you a lot, believe me!"

"You think an old lady can't see things well anymore and can't hear things. I know what's going on in the East, I know that people are wanted and I know that your family is in danger. I'm not fooled, my boy," she said kindly.

"Madam, we are good people..." he tried to explain to her, before being interrupted.

"I'm not done. You don't interrupt an old lady," she smiled at him. "In my life, I have also learned to believe in what I see and what I see is that you and your love are good people. Even though you have come to find refuge, you bring much joy to an old woman who has never been able to have children. This village hears but is not interested in what is happening in our poor world. Despite the consequences, we are poor in every way, and nothing will change what we are. Here you are safe. People will not say anything, because they are not interested. You can make a new life here. My house is now yours. I want you to inherit what I have, it is not much I'm afraid, but a life."

Samuel did not know what to say. He finally saw his life, a life for Honoré and him. He took her hand.

"You make me a happy man, and I don't know what to say. I have nothing to offer you but a simple thank you."

"You are mistaken, young man. Marry her tomorrow! ask Honoré to marry you. That will make an old lady a bit lively."

He thought this was a wonderful idea, and smiled.

"I'll ask her right away. Thank you, ma'am. Will I finally know your name?"

"I lost my name a long time ago, a time that is behind me. I don't need a name to be happy. Old lady is enough for me. Go, now!"

He ran off, found Honoré in the garden, and stopped to admire her. She got up exhausted by the heat, wiped her forehead before seeing him and giving him a beautiful smile. He ran to embrace her.

"I love you Honoré," he said, taking her by the hip.

"Did the sun hit you on the head?" she laughed at him, and looked at him in love.

"Maybe so," he knelt down, and he stammered before beginning. "Today is a special day, the day of hope, of a new life. I wanted to tell you that I love you and that I would like to love you all my life. Would you like me? Would you like a small life near me but filled with the beauty of our love?"

She looked at him without a word. He didn't know what it meant. He was trying to guess. Then she hugged him, sobbing.

"Yes my love, of course! It took you a long time!" she hugged him as if it was their first hug. "Glad to hear it. Tomorrow morning at dawn, let's get married. The old lady has it all planned."

They kissed, and then he stayed to help her, for most of the afternoon.

It was one of the best moments of their lives. They laughed and teased each other, as if time had stopped.

Later that evening, he returned to the duties that now served his own. If a part of his heart was broken, he understood that his choices, like his father's choices, always carry a consequence and that he would have to live with it.

Happy, the day passed quickly. He was now looking forward to the morning. They did not sleep in the same room. According to tradition, the bride and groom had to take a vow of abstinence for the night before the wedding, in order to prepare themselves for a life together.

As daylight was about to break, Samuel stepped out onto the porch. The old lady was already waiting with an older man, a witness, as they are called.

They are designated according to their maturity, to be able to marry a couple. He greeted them. Samuel suddenly became anxious.

Then the sun came out of its hiding place, along with his beloved. The old lady knew how to handle the needle. Although the fabric was old and tarnished, Honoré was splendid. The dress, with its flower crown, showed her off to her best advantage.

She came forward, her eyes shining. At the height of happiness, they did not stop looking at each other.

A few minutes later, they were joined, husband and wife. They spent the day in bed, eating and giggling until they were dizzy. Samuel had never copulated so much since he was with a woman and had never loved in such a way.

The next day he went fishing at dawn. He was happy, he felt like his life was really starting.

He passed a group of men, men too well dressed to be native to this village. Maybe it was nothing, just men trying to intimidate weaker men than themselves, but as a precaution, he stuck his head in his hood.

Samuel was always wary. He knew the little man wouldn't let them go anytime soon, and worse, he wanted them dead. They stared at him without questioning him.

During the day, Samuel eventually forgot about them, as his joy could not fade away.

After his day, he went straight home to the old lady, as usual, without passing through the village. He didn't want to attract any looks or suspicion.

The further they stayed from civilization, the safer they were. As he approached, he sensed danger. A cloud of smoke was floating around their home.

His heart stopped. Dropping the fish net he ran as fast as he could.

The house was burning. Samuel shouted Honoré's name as loud as he could, but received no answer. Panicked, he went around the house, and discovered the old woman hanging with her hands cut off, on the threshold of the back door.

He fell to his knees thinking that Honoré had been burned to death, her child with her. He was crushed, and cried out in pain. Suddenly the group of men appeared through the undergrowth. One of them challenged him.

"Your wife is delicious, but I didn't teach you anything?" he was laughing hard.

Samuel got up and hit him in the face.

The man retaliated and left him on the ground. He signaled to the others who brought Honoré to them half-conscious.

"We were waiting for you. But don't worry, we took good care of her, and she didn't get bored. Now that we are complete, you will watch her die."

They laughed loudly, Samuel wanted to give him another shot, but two acolytes firmly prevented him.

Finally immobilized, one of the men took out his broad-bladed knife and cut the hands of the beautiful Honoré before slitting her throat, as gently as possible.

Samuel screamed, powerless, blocked by these mercenaries. His anger was immense.

Finally, the men let go of their embrace. Samuel collapsed, then rose to his feet, struck the assailants who had reduced him to impotence, grabbed a sword and headed for Honoré's killer. Hit by an arrow in the thigh, he got up with difficulty, but his hatred was even more painful. He wanted justice. He wanted this man dead. He received a second one in the other leg. He got up, and swung his sword at the man but missed.

The man took advantage of this opportunity to hit him in the head. He was not faint but only stunned, so between half reality and half nightmare.

He saw there, in this fatal fate, the responsibility of his sister Lia. He felt betrayed. He had the feeling that if she was not what she was, Honoré would still be alive. Those men would not have been so hard on them.

He was taken before the little man. Wounded, he hoped more than anything to die. The world, his life and his family were disgusting to him, but a child's sobbing brought him back to reality, and reattached him to life.

It was Annie, Honoré's daughter, so she was alive.

The little man took her, looked at her, kissed her and then smiled at Samuel.

"Do you care about this child?"

"Of course," he was struggling.

"Good, because I have a proposition to make to you and if you accept, you will stay alive with this child, or rather with what you have left of your lost love."

Then he laughed, a rude, thunderous laugh that Samuel would never forget. Never again would he let people hurt him.

He made a promise to Honoré, wherever she was, to protect the child she had given birth to as if it were his own. And for that, he was ready to change and forget his past.

He was willing to become another man to keep his last promise.

18

A disappeared people

*I*n the middle of the forest, Emile stopped and turned to them.

"I'm sorry, but from here on out, I have to blindfold you. The area we are about to enter is a secret lair, and only the faithful are allowed to know the way."

"What? It's out of the question," retorted Kéo, "Lia, it smells like an ambush!"

"I didn't come all the way here for nothing. I will go all the way!"

"In this case, we follow you," answered Rose by throwing a glance to Kéo.

"Some guards are already there. Once blindfolded, they will help me guide you."

Kéo and Rose looked around worriedly. When Emile approached Rose to put the blindfold on, Kéo snatched it out of his hands, challenging him with his eyes. He blindfolded Rose himself and instead of letting Emile do it. Then Emile approached Lia.

"Don't worry. I'll drive you," he said to her.

"I'm not worried," she said cautiously.

Emile gently pushed her forward, and at the same time, she heard stealthy footsteps slowly approaching them. Probably the guards. As she moved forward, a thousand questions raced through her mind. It seemed to her that the road lasted for hours. The silence between them became heavy and even suffocating. She began to doubt her decisions, and fear gnawed at her at the idea of putting her friends in danger.

A few steps further on, they stopped. Emile put her on one knee and whispered to her.

"Formality. Don't be afraid."

The blindfold was removed, and the sudden light made it impossible for her to see clearly.

After a few seconds she began to see more definite shapes. She finally perceived the place where they had arrived.

They were in the middle of a huge forest, the trees were gigantic, the buildings were not built on the ground, but on top of the trees. They were made of wood with footbridges that connected the trees to facilitate the passage. To go up there, it was necessary to borrow splendid staircases braided of lianas of wood. The steps were strewn with grasses and flowers. At first glance, there were no flaws. Perfection flowed from all sides. The show did not end there.

Shrubs, and flowers of all colors embalmed the landscape. Even the grass was perfect, soft and regular. Lia could not see one smaller or larger than the other.

Sparkling white benches were set up everywhere.

The panorama became even more magical as the sun fell. The lit torches gave a golden glow that enhanced the beauty of the landscape.

Soft, melodious music whispered in her ears as if to lull her to sleep. Birds with bright black wings whistled this sound. The song of a brook came to harmonize with this melody, a waterfall overhung the forest, and snaked between the trees.

Wooden bridges went from bank to bank. Lia and her friends stood at the only place completely surrounded by the river, facing a majestic tree, taller than all the others.

Something resembling a man came to join Emile. It was not human. They seemed to come straight out of fairy tales.

As they did so, others approached and stared at them. They were tall, with long golden-blond hair. They had small black eyes, and a rosy complexion that brought out their thin, perfectly shaped lips. Their ears were pointed and thin.

The men-like creatures were dressed in green, similar to the leaves of the trees. They had a top with three-quarter cut sleeves, a V-shaped slit, tight-fitting pants, and black boots.

The women-like creatures were dressed in a white tunic, and golden strings, as straps, held the dress on the shoulders and arms. They wore white ballerinas decorated with golden beads. Some had a black ribbon that highlighted their long blonde hair, and others had their hair loose with a black rose tucked into the corner of their ear.

Her friends were now on their knees, and Lia felt embarrassed by all the stares. Kéo and Rose looked at them in fear.

A man walked towards them. He was older than the others, but he was as robust as a man of twenty. He looked at them sternly.

"We were waiting for you! I have to say that I thought you were much more, how shall I say, impressive and maybe prettier."

Lia did not say a word. To tell the truth, she didn't understand what she was doing there. She looked at Emile who winked at her. She wanted to get up, but the man prevented her from doing so and fixed her with a hard look.

"In the presence of our sovereigns, newcomers must remain on land as a mark of respect. The sovereigns are the only ones who consent to your presence."

"And if not?" challenged Kéo.

"In that case, it's exile," the man replied with a wry half-smile.

"In that case, it's fine with me," Kéo was smiling at Lia. He preferred that to staying longer with these strangers.

"If I were you, I would not wish it. Exile in these lands is certain death. Unless you were born there and are a warrior, would you be one by chance?"

Suddenly, facing Lia, the crowd parted to let two people enter the heart of the circle.

A man and a woman, with the same physiognomy as the others. On closer inspection, they were taller, their outfits touched the ground, and their ornaments were much lighter than their golden hair and brought out their azure blue eyes.

The woman embodied gentleness, while the man exuded severity and intransigence, which did not bode well. The man was imposing, and charismatic and yet, seemed familiar to Lia. Had she seen him before? In a dream? She could not remember. The heavy atmosphere prevented her from thinking.

He looked at her for a few minutes before saying these words.

" I am King Solis, and this is Queen Luna. We are the people of the earth elves, and we live on what the earth calls itself, Iotopia. We have been waiting for you for a long time. You must have a thousand questions, but at the moment I cannot answer them. My kingdom is in trouble, and I must retire for a while. When I return, we will talk. In the meantime, be welcome. As a formality, you must know some of the laws of our people. Cordis will train you in our ways, "he said, pointing to the man who had spoken earlier. "He will take you to Papilio, the oldest and wisest of us. He is our memory. See you soon, Lia."

They walked away from their people. As a sign of respect, each one placed their hand over their heart. Everyone left with furtive glances in their direction. Lia couldn't say a word. She didn't know where she had arrived, who these people were, and what they wanted from her. Emile motioned for them to get up and together they followed Cordis. He walked briskly but elegantly.

They walked around a tree to cross a bridge. After a few steps, he took them up a staircase to the top of a different tree.

As she climbed the steps, Lia remembered the beauty of the landscape. From up there, everything was even more splendid. As she walked slowly, lost in her reverie in front of such a spectacle, Cordis cleared his throat to make her move. He stopped at the first door and entered. Emile took Lia's arm.

"I will wait for you here. I am not allowed to stay. You can't enter the sanctuary unless you're invited."

Her face betrayed her disappointment and concern. Emile noticed immediately, and reassured her.

"Don't worry. I can assure you that you are safe here. It's just a few rules, stupid in my opinion, but their rules. And you'll already have some answers. The wise old man is a learned man."

He gave her a last smile and walked away. She walked in. The room had no windows. The light came from the flowers that covered the ceiling. Foliage climbed along the shelves and tables, and the floor was covered with grass, like a soft, cool carpet.

The landmark was a library, the place was filled with books from floor to ceiling, and stairs surrounded the shelves. The few tables were the same white color as the furniture she had seen outside.

Rose and Kéo were sitting at a table away from an elderly man.

He was not like the others, he was small, wrinkled, without hair and he had no ears. He stood up with the help of a cane and walked towards Lia.

"You must be Lia. Follow me!"

Cordis looked at them, then away to the back of the room. Lia followed the man to a strange shelf with a door and a snake as a handle.

As the man put his hand on it, the snake seemed to moan louder and louder. Suddenly, it started to move. It was alive! It unwound and disappeared behind the furniture. Papilio looked at her astonished air.

"It is part of what we call *the guardians*. Many animals or elements that inhabit our planet are here to protect certain things that must be protected. This one sees deep inside you. They only open the door to pure hearts, those who want good. Otherwise, its bite is deadly!"

Lia was still silent. He handed her a parchment and beckoned her to sit with him. He began his speech loud enough for her friends to hear as well.

"The scroll you are holding is called *Quaero*. You and your friends will have to sign it. Of course, it will be signed only if you agree to the terms. You see, this is a special scroll. Once you put your name on it, it allows you to find any person wherever he or she is. Well, let's get started! You must be curious about who we are and why we are hidden from the world. You see, a long time ago, all people lived together. In spite of many difficulties due to their different beliefs, we still came to a certain trust. For years, we walked side by side, where man is destroying himself today. One day, a tragedy occurred, a man greedy for more power unleashed the darkness and with it, the destruction of the Earth. Our people, like others, withdrew. As for the man, he grew up for years in loneliness, disarray and violence. One day, he was reformed, hope was reborn, but man, always wanting more power, made the world fall back into darkness. You have lived in this darkness. The other peoples no longer wanted to meddle in the affairs of men, but preferred to remain hidden. With time, men forgot our existence, making us look like creatures from fairy tales."

"So, if I understand correctly, you have abandoned us," Lia replied highly.

"You may see it that way, but you have not experienced darkness. Even we would have been hurt if we had stayed. Man unleashed something that no one could control. There was no question of paying the price for man's madness. Were we right or wrong? That is not the question anymore. Everyone makes

226

choices in their lives to protect what they believe is right. For some, it is far from being right. No one can blame a decision that was made with heart. Cruel or not."

"So what am I doing here? You decide today to help us?" she asked sharply.

"These questions are not for me to answer. I am here to give you some safety rules. Our lands are populated with creatures, more or less ferocious. We must know some of them to approach them and others to flee from. So I recommend that you only go out if your life is in danger or if you are with someone more experienced than yourself. There are many peoples. Whatever your motives are, you can't disclose them to humans. There would be great losses on both sides. Well, we have a second strict rule; never pick our roses! A faithful person can only pick them. Elves are not like in your stories. They are neither nice nor mean, but beware little one, if a rule is broken, it is the banishment that awaits you. You see, the elves have codes, those of honor and respect, something you will have to abide by if you want to live with us."

"There must be a misunderstanding. I never intended to stay. I have a family waiting for me. I came for help."

"So, in this case you are in the wrong place!" interrupted Cordis and replied sternly, "our people don't like men. In no way will they help!"

"So why bring me in?"

"The king knows your mother."

Lia was speechless. So her mother knows this place.

"How did she know him? I don't understand, what do you want from me?" she continued to ask.

"It's up to king Solis to tell you more," Cordis continued dryly.

"I don't have time to wait, my family is in danger."

"The only choice you have is to wait!" he paused before continuing. "We are done. Emile will take care of you. Sign out now." Cordis turned his back on her with disdain.

Papilio approached her and took her hand.

"I'm glad I met you. I've been waiting a long time. Your mother was a wonderful person. Come back and see me. You are welcome here."

Then he turned around. Lia signed first. For her, everything was confusing, so signing a piece of paper wasn't so bad. Emile was waiting at the door. Kéo and Rose were silent from the beginning. Rose said:

"How is it possible that such things exist? Nothing is clear Lia. I don't feel safe."

"They didn't really answer our questions either, what are you going to do?" continued Kéo, afraid of the turn of the situation.

"I have no choice but to stay. I don't know how to help my family, I need these people to help me. I will wait for the return of their king. What about you?" she peered at everyone, one by one.

"We stay too," said Kéo, "we have nowhere else to go. You are still our family," he put his hand on her shoulder.

"Good," smiled Emile, who had joined them. "Anyway, once you stay long enough, you get used to this place, I assure you."

"Is that who you do business with?" asked Lia.

"Yes, among others. As I said, I deal with whoever needs it, I can assure you one thing, you are safer here than at home. They won't hurt you, most of the time, and as long as the rules are followed, they are peaceful. They are great warriors and even agile, having fought alongside them before. If you win their hearts, you will have an advantage, Lia."

"What do you know about them?" she continued to ask.

"Enough to give them my trust. They let me sleep here, and eat but I only share those two things. They're pretty secretive when you're not part of their community. Now, let's get some rest. The place where I sleep, has two other rooms."

Emile led them to a tree house. Kéo and Rose didn't even bother to eat and went to bed immediately. Lia sat down at the table and Emile gave her something to eat. He looked at her for a moment.

"Are you afraid?"

"To tell you the truth, I don't know. Everything is so confusing. But strangely, I feel connected to this place. I can't say why. And then I keep thinking about my family. Maybe they are going through a terrible time while I am lucky enough to be resting peacefully in a soft bed!"

"Don't worry. We'll find a solution when the time comes." He paused, and reached into his jacket to hand her a flower. "Here, they give it to brave women."

"Brave? I wouldn't describe myself that way!"

"You may not see it, but I do."

He took her face in his hands and kissed her. She had been dreading this moment. In the end, it was sweeter and more enjoyable than she thought. Deep inside, she had longed for it. Her heart was beating so fast. They looked at each other for a moment, undecided, she wondered what to do. Against all expectations, at the moment when he was going to leave, she kissed him in her turn. She wanted to feel loved and appreciated.

They kissed there, languidly. Then, staring at each other for a moment, they delicately released their embrace.

"I have to sleep, thanks Emile … for everything!" she looked into his eyes, and felt her face turning red.

"Thanks to you, you are the first person who gives me this smile. Have a good rest," he took her hand one more time, before letting her go.

19

To other secrets

*L*ia woke up early and discovered that the main room was empty. She noticed breakfast on the table and an envelope with her name on it. Emile must have made her breakfast and left her the note. It read,

Lia,

Thank you for the evening. As I write this, you are fast asleep. I didn't want to wake you up, so I'm taking the trouble to write you these few words. As you read them, I am already gone for two or three days, not more. Work is calling me, but I know that when I come back, you will be here. In the meantime, try to enjoy what's around you. It's worth it, believe me. Open your eyes to this New World and live!   Emile.

She put the letter down, finished eating and decided to take his advice. She had few options anyway and conceded that, for now, it was best to wait.

When she came out of the fireplace, the sun was starting to rise. The place was magical, and she couldn't get enough of it. She went downstairs to look around. Attracted by the waterfall, she sat down for a moment at the water's edge.

A woman, an elf, of course, walked towards her.

"Hello stranger," she said with an angelic voice.

"Hello!" Lia replied agedly.

"I saw you at the welcoming ceremony. I know you are new. With Emile gone, I was assigned to be your guide. Would you like me to show you around?"

"With pleasure," Lia answered her smiling.

This was the perfect opportunity for her to learn more about these people. They walked without a word, at first, until they approached what looked like a market.

"Here we make all sorts of potions, and weapons, and, in our greatest secrecy, we grow roses."

"Why are they so special?"

"This is our secret, by definition. You humans think of them as mere decoration, but they are much more than that. Every creation on earth is a blessing. We are here to preserve them. Everything is energy, even the smallest thing. If you learn to look, you will discover more than meets the eye. It is here that our differences and our visions of life, reside. It is everyone's duty to respect what allows us to live. Like what we eat. By thanking it for feeding us, we give back to the earth a new energy that allows a new cycle and thus preserves nature. When we take, we must always give something. Even with a word, they are an incredible force of energy. "

' What if we don't?" Lia was not sure that she understood.

"One day, sooner or later, there are consequences, an illness, a loss... That's fate. Life is like that. We come to life out of love and we have the task of staying in it, and it is through it that we find the answers, and it is it that guides us."

"Love does not solve everything. No matter how much we love, sometimes it's not enough!"

"Bad experiences exist to help us to evolve. Nothing is easy, but if we love and stay on our path, everything will be better!"

Lia did not want to hear anymore, a part of her was too hurt, and she changed the conversation.

"Do you use plants? And what for?"

"Come, I'll show you."

She walked toward a recess that didn't look like a dwelling. It was dark, like a cave. This one was covered with foliage of various colors.

The young woman asked her to wait and returned with some grass.

"Several kinds of potions can be made, but some should not be mixed together."

"I still don't know your name," intervened Lia, curious about her new friend."

"They call me Eleftería."

"Why are you so nice to me? Am I not a stranger to you, a stranger not to be trusted?"

"Among my people, I am different. I aspire to so much more than the destiny I have been chosen for. I respect our values, but I am not afraid of the future or the unknown. I think it's right to show you who we are, if you want to fit in."

At these words, she did not answer anything. Although she was grateful for her kindness. There was no question of staying too long away from her homeland.

But, for Lia, Elefthería was right about one thing. She needed to know more about these new people if she was to win them over.

The day was fruitful. Lia learned about the plants, and on this occasion, discovered more about the mysterious people.

As she walked back to the cabin, she passed an individual who looked like a man. He was shaved on the sides of his head and had black hair. She didn't know if his eyes were deceiving her, but they were red in the sunlight. He was not very tall, although Lia was small herself. When he turned his eyes toward her, she shivered. It wasn't fear, but it was indescribable. She looked away and hurried toward her friends.

When she returned to the hut, Kéo and Rose were sitting by the table talking in low voices. When they saw Lia, they stopped.

"Have you been locked up all day? Why not take advantage of what's going on outside? It's worth it, believe me," Lia said while placing the bouquet of plants that she gathered on the table.

"What is happening to you, Lia?" asked Rose.

"Yes, it's true. This is not our home. They are monsters! They are not like us. Talk to the king and let's follow your plan," Kéo eagerly said, dismissing the bouquet of flowers.

"I DIDN'T FORGET IT!" she replied coldly. "But what to do? To remain to mope? My father didn't raise me like that. I didn't think you were like that, Kéo! Anyway, King Solis isn't here. Would you like to go back home without finding a way to help the people we love? It's eating away at me to stay and have fun, but we don't have a choice and it's not a solution either to stay and do nothing. I want you to know that today I learned things that humans don't know about the richness of plants. And I believe that this can be useful! Stop your childish whims. I won't allow you to say that it doesn't affect me to stay here!"

They looked at each other without a word and Lia got up to get something to eat.

"Sorry," Kéo muttered, looking down at the floor, "It's just that I feel useless." His eyes finally caught Lia's, "I keep thinking about the ones we lost. I feel guilty for being alive when hundreds have died. You're probably right. Being locked up in this hut doesn't help, but I'm afraid. Yes, I am afraid. Lia, these people … everything is insane and unimaginable at the same time. It's all so foreign to us that it makes me feel unsafe. But I promise to make an effort and to integrate."

Lia nodded, not knowing what to say. She was as frightened as he was by the whole situation. His unanswered questions were confusing her. And above all, she was not very good with patience.

"I think Emile is right. They're not evil, they're very good at a lot of things and they have a lot of knowledge about what's around them," said Lia trying to calm down the atmosphere. "I think that can be beneficial for our future war. I can't do anything now but at least I'm learning. I saw a training camp, and they want me to train."

"Really? Don't you think it's weird," Rose replied.

"Weird? Why is that?"

"Emile told us that they never integrate strangers into their business, especially humans," explained Rose.

"This is surely a good omen. Maybe they will help us." Lia said, not sure either.

"I hope you're right," Kéo mused.

Lia spent the rest of the day in the presence of the elves. She could feel that her friends were still bothered and upset and she desperately wanted to steer away from any more arguments. It was time to calm down, each in his own way.

The next morning, as she was about to go out, Kéo caught up with her.

"I'll come with you, I need to move."

They crossed the forest together. Most of the inhabitants were already up and about. Lia had noticed the day before that the elves moved with great elegance and grace. They were also surprisingly calm. One would think that nothing could disturb them.

In the distance, Eleftería was busy collecting empty baskets. When she saw Lia, she waved to her.

"Good morning! I hope you had a good rest. I will guide you to the training ground."

As they approached, they could just about hear the blades graze each other. Kéo, amazed by their skill with weapons, barely moved. A man pushed him and did not bother to apologize.

"We usually have good manners. Ekaitz is a royal guard, so he can be a bit pretentious. Don't take it personally."

"Yes I noticed. There are some things you need to learn from humans!" replied Kéo casually.

Lia glared at him for his remark. Eleftería laughed, and did not seem offended. She pointed to an elf, who showed them the rest of the day's fighting. Kéo, although reluctant, let himself be dragged into the frantic duels.

They returned back to the hut exhausted. Rose had already cooked. Lia smiled showing off her thin facial features as she sat down.

"It's like old times," Lia said.

"Except that we are not at home!" Kéo's voice sounded desperate.

"Recognize that their knowledge exceeds ours."

"I admit that the day was rewarding."

With these words, Lia finished her dinner and went to bed. Although she was still sad about the recent events. The day with these new people made her happy. She had always wanted to explore the world and now she had an opportunity before her. The elves, different from her people, had a way of seeing the world that Lia liked. That night as she rested into her slumber, she did not have a nightmare.

Lia was awakened by a racket. She looked out the window and spotted the elves waving around in a frightened manner. Kéo, half awake, followed by Rose, stood beside her.

"But what's going on? What's all this noise?" asked a puzzled Kéo.

"I don't know, but it sounds like something bad is happening. I'll go check it out."

"We're coming with you," exclaimed Rose.

Downstairs, guards were gathering, and women were busy bringing in weapons and ammunition. It looked like a war was brewing.

Cordis ran towards them, serious as usual.

"It's not time to daydream. Follow me!"

They followed him without a word. Neither Lia nor her friends wanted to argue with him.

"Let's see, faster! I have more urgent things to do," says Cordis, impatiently.

He stopped dead in his tracks, in front of the same tree as when they arrived. He walked towards the den.

"Well, you must remember the way?! Join Papilio!"

Then, without another word, he turned his back on them and left. They watched him walk away.

"Let's go find our answers," said Lia pushing the door.

Papilio threw himself on her.

"Lia, I was waiting for you. Come here, let's hurry. We don't have much time."

"What's going on?" a vein started to throb in Lia's forehead.

"The hour is serious, very serious. A war is about to break out and with it, yours!"

"Mine? It started a while ago," she continued to say without understanding the situation.

"Wait a minute! Did you say a war?" replied Rose worriedly.

"Yes, you heard me right, I'm afraid."

"Lia," said Kéo. "We just left one and we find another? And then, why take part in it? I don't even know these people!"

"Children! Don't look so panicked! Do you think we'll leave the most vulnerable at the enemy's mercy? See, there is a well-hidden and secure place. Let's all go there!"

"Another place?" repeated Rose in fear.

Lia turned to Papilio.

"If we're going to follow you, we need to know what's going on. The mysteries must end!" her gaze to him was serious and determined.

Lia sat down, Rose and Kéo were at her side. Papilio looked at them a moment. In front of their determined and implacable faces, he sat down in his turn and took a breath before speaking.

"You're right, if it's going to be your war too..."

" What?" gasped Kéo, but Lia motioned for him to be quiet.

"When we all fled your land, evil things followed in our wake. Perhaps this is our fate? Although this island is home to dangerous creatures that could be compared to your animals, like lions or bears. There are unpredictable beasts. They are not so easily domesticated, although some manage to do so. In your eyes they are monsters, while most of the time they protect themselves to survive. There are several kinds of creatures; some are aggressive only to protect their territory. Others have evil intentions, having come into the world to destroy. An evil in our land is growing, some people are seeking to gain more power. The course of history has always been like this. You were born Lia, with this kind of person. The ugly ones, they are called druids. Although the druids have sworn to protect the weakest, some use their knowledge for evil. They have more or less power. They control the beasts, and force the weakest by transforming them into abominable things. One of them has declared war. It is not one of the most powerful but it is important to stop this kind of person once and for all. You see, we have some wealth, some knowledge that could be used to destroy everything good on this earth.

It is vital to stop him, because every people has their own secrets. If he manages to unravel all these mysteries, your war would be nothing compared to what will happen. On his side he already has a powerful army. He controls the manticores, creatures with the lion's body, the tail of a scorpion, and wings. They kill everything they see. Then he has black elves, created by a man named Orion. He was power hungry, and his greed eventually caused him to be banished from his people, the earth elves. He developed a grudge against man that grew and grew. Many times he quarreled with King Solis. One day he crossed a line that he should not have crossed. He killed one of his own. Refusing to sentence him to death, King Solis banished him forever. He felt betrayed and rejected, then took refuge in a cave where he lived in the wild. He promised to take revenge. Two years passed, when everyone thought he was dead, a druid found him, thinned out, his eyes yellow with hatred. He helped Orion create the dark elves. With time, he changed his appearance, and his skin became black, but he kept his blond hair which he cut very short. Since that day, what little soul he had left has disappeared forever. One day, he declared war on the other elves, and during a battle, he killed his own sister, removing all traces of his past. With this gesture, he showed that he no longer feared anything. It was years of war. All the peoples united with King Solis. Orion lost the war. No one saw him or his people anymore. Some thought he was dead. But let's get back to what concerns us; a few days ago, some elves disappeared. One of the elf trackers saw an army of dark elves. Orion is not dead and walks beside the druid."

"Does this druid have a name?" asked Lia.

"Arzel," he said frantically.

"I would like to help," Lia said. "I don't want to be left behind this time."

Kéo and Rose stared at her.

"Have you lost your mind," said Rose.

"Let's stop talking and get ready to go to the den! It's safe, right?" Kéo scanned Papilios face.

"Yes, don't worry!" said Papilio.

Lia turned back to her friends, determined to do something good, she couldn't help her family, but at least she could do something that could change some people's lives.

"I understand your worries. This place is full of mysteries. It's so sudden and new. I will not leave without getting the answers I am looking for. We are trying to change things for our country, and fear is something we know. It destroys everything, even what's inside of us. I have to do something. I need to do something. Let me do what I think is right!"

They looked at her for a moment, then Kéo stared her down.

"You are right! Although I'm not alone," turning to Rose, "the woman I love stands beside me. Let's not change who we are. I'll come with you!"

"What?" screamed Rose in fear.

Kéo turned to her and took her hands.

"You know I've always been a warrior, you know everything about me. If Lia goes, I won't be the coward who turns his back. I want you to make me a promise, to follow these people no matter what."

She looked at him, and nodded before they both fell into each other's arms.

"Well," says Papilio, "that saves me a useless talk. Indeed, Lia you can help, but not in the way you think. The elves won't let you fight alongside them, they only fight with people who have shown their trust. Emile went in search of a powerful weapon. He was joined by warriors called the Korrigans. In the old days, they were dwarves, but little by little their species has changed because of their closeness to the human people. Their appearance has changed, they are now more like a man, although some are still unpleasant. Most of them are tall. From their former people, they have kept themselves generous but at the same time they have a fearsome personality, if they feel betrayed. They have always had beautiful hair and red eyes, but depending on their mood, they change color. Having them on our side would be an advantage. Find them, warn them that war is coming. We have no time to lose, and above all, don't tell anyone about what you are about to do. On the road, I will signal you the right moment to leave. The advantage of war is that no one will pay attention to you."

"But how would I know where to find them?"

"Do you remember the papyrus I made you sign? I'll give you Emile's. It will guide you to him. Lia listen carefully, although I wanted to come with you to warn you of dangers unknown to you, you must be extremely careful. What lies outside is an unknown world, sometimes fierce. I will provide you with weapons. Remember these words if you feel in danger *Some of nature's creations, though their appearances are frightening, are far more frightened by your presence!"*

A few minutes later, they were already on their way to the city of Nube, the refuge. On the way, they were all silent. The fear of the women was felt by Lia who was the only one who could understand them. The impossibility of not being able to control things was difficult to accept.

They had stopped for a while when Kéo told her that Papilio had signaled them. He had a bag full of provisions with him.

Silently, Lia unrolled the paper, which began to shimmer, and letters began to change shape to make way for a map. They armed themselves with the bows provided by Papillo, then continued on their way.

In two days, they had to find Emile, hoping to return in time.

20

The mission

Kéo bent over the river to fill their water bottles. They had been on the road for more than a day. They were about to leave, after stopping for the night. Although everyone had warned them that this forest was dangerous, they had not encountered anything scary so far.

Lia was sitting on a rock when Kéo joined her.

"The sooner we finish, the sooner we will be safe."

"I don't see what you're afraid of, the forest doesn't seem threatening at all," she noticed, looking around.

"Just because you can't see something doesn't mean we shouldn't be on guard. This forest is evil. Have you noticed anything strange?"

"No, nothing!" she was looked around carefully this time.

"Exactly nothing! Not a sound, listen! Not a bird, not a rabbit, not an animal on the prowl... For over a day, nothing. You can hardly hear the wind blowing. There is something wrong, Lia," he glanced around, but with fear.

"Now that you mention it, it's strange," she took the map to find her bearings before leaving. "We are not very far. It is strange. Emile did not move since we followed him. Let's go and get it this over with"

This time they walked away much faster. They no longer spoke, but were preoccupied with listening to what was happening around them. Suddenly, as Lia walked ahead, Kéo shouted.

"RUN, RUN!"

Without even trying to understand, she started to run alongside Kéo.

The only thing she heard was the footsteps of a beast chasing them. It sounded like a bear. Lia was almost sure, it sounded exactly like her sister Georgina's bears.

She stumbled and fell down a steep hill. Recovering from her emotions, she hid behind a bush, listening for Kéo's footsteps.

Hearing nothing, she began to pick up her weapons and moved silently forward, fearful of seeing the beast again.

As she walked, she realized that her ankle was hurting so much that she could only limp along.

A few minutes later, still no trace, neither of Kéo nor of the beast. She couldn't turn back. The slope was too steep and with her ankle in this condition, she wouldn't be able to climb it. Although she had learned to recognize the tracks left of an animal on the ground, she still lacked practice.

Thinking she was lost, she stopped at a river to cool off and rest her leg for a few minutes. She winced as she discovered her swollen ankle. She wondered how much longer she could walk. She tried to cheer up as her younger sister Georgina would have done.

At this thought, the memory of her sister drawing resurfaced, the laughter of her sisters echoed in her heart. She suddenly remembered the sketch Georgina had drawn a few months earlier and realized that she had reproduced King Solis's likeness. Although she was sure that Georgina had never met him before, it could not be a coincidence. When she returned to *Iotopia,* she would have to solve this mystery.

She got up and walked with a determined step, despite the pain. As she crossed the river, something bright caught her eye. She followed it, but it was moving very fast. As she tried to keep up, she realized that she was at a dead end.

An impressive number of trees blocked any passage. Seeing no way to cross, she decided to turn back. As a dark thought crossed her mind, a gust of wind forced her to turn around.

Through the trees, she saw a light. At first distant, then closer and closer, it kept spinning around, drawing quick little circles in the air, as if inviting Lia to follow it. She had a strange feeling, the more she looked at it, the more she felt at peace. On her way, the trees were moving, but that did not worry her.

A few steps further on and she landed on a hill. From above, she could see an endless field of flowers, around giant trees that joined together to form a gigantic circle. A kind of hut made of roses and flowers stood near a river. Not far from there, children were playing, climbing a cliff and then sliding down it.

As Lia approached, she saw that people were coming out of the trees, which were actually houses. The blue light landed on a tree, to anchor itself in its roots.

Closer ... closer and Lia discovered that the luminous halo had the shape of a small woman, like a fairy no bigger than a hand. The fairies legs took root, becoming one with the tree.

"Who..." Lia cleared her throat, "Who are you?"

"I belong to the dryads, people of nature."

"I thought that was reserved for elves."

"We are nothing like the elves. We are Nature, and we exist only through her. We move only through her," she said, carrying a consistent tone as she spoke. At that moment, Lia lost sight of her. She disappeared and reappeared closer to her. She moved, as if gliding on the grass and her legs came to take root in it.

"You see, we are one with nature. We are their words."

"Which sides are you on? Are you there to help?"

"We are neither for one nor for the other. We act accordingly to the present and help what needs to be helped. But we only help the most seasoned. You see, these children, they live here because we helped their parents."

"Where are they?" she glanced around, hoping to see more people.

"These trees are their homes," she pointed in the direction of the big trees, down the hill. "They are in a peaceful environment, no violence and no form of aggression reigns here."

Lia listened carefully, even though this place seemed serene, it did not seem legitimate to her to suppress certain emotions that were an integral part of the men. Although sometimes he acts out of revenge or love. Our actions are a reflection of our existence, trying at every moment to improve ourselves for a better life. What is a life, if we only feel it halfway? she kept thinking.

"Why did you lead me here?" Lia was puzzled. "Are you worried about being a prisoner?" she asked serenely, before pursuing. "In this case, there is no need to fear. You cannot be part of this community, although your heart is noble. Your quest will serve at all, and I am one more light in your path. You were heading towards something uncontrollable and dangerous. And in your state, it is impossible for you to fight."

"You mean the beast that scared my friend and me? Do you know where he is?"

"I do, but this is far too dangerous. Your quest must continue. We can lead you as quickly as possible to your friend, the one who pushed you to come here."

"I won't leave without Kéo," she said, trying to control her tone.

"In that case, here, take this fruit," she pointed in direction of a tree. "It is very powerful, and can put anyone to sleep."

"Where is my friend?" She asked as she gently removed the fruit from the tree. It was much heavier than she thought.

"I will show you the way, but beware. What is after you has a lot of strength. Your friend is still alive, for he had the good sense to climb the trees. But that won't hold the beast for long."

"How do you know that?"

"We can see anyone through nature, be it a tree or a flower. First, approach this river, and dip your ankle in it."

Lia complied. In just a moment, her ankle swelled and the pain faded until it disappeared completely. She gazed at her in amazement.

"We have infinite gifts. But we must be careful, they could turn against anyone who uses them excessively!"

"You mean it's dangerous to use such powers? And yet, it could help so many people!" she said disapprovingly.

"Good luck, Lia!" she cut her off without even taking the time to answer her, and changed back into a ball of light.

Lia didn't remember giving her name. The dryad must be powerful enough to help her find her family, she thought.

She then showed her the path she had to take and disappeared. She assumed that danger was near.

She walked at a snail's pace, then she heard a noise, a growl that would make even the bravest of people shudder. The closer she got, the more the ground seemed to move.

She heard Kéo screaming. She had heard him shout like that before, to give himself courage or to face danger, when they were hunting together. He told her that, in the past, the warriors of his village used to shout. It meant courage for them.

As she got closer she saw the massive beast. It must have been four times the size of Kéo. It looked like a bear, except for a few details; if its body was comparable to a bear, although it was bigger, its head and hands looked like an owl's. Its eyes, with each attack, became blacker and madness could be read in them.

Lia crouched down and quickly thought of an attack approach. She used her bow to attract the beast's attention, drumming on trees and puddles. With a burst of anger, the animal turned toward Lia.

Roaring, it got up on all fours and dashed furiously in her direction. Lia threw a few arrows at him, but to no avail. His thick fur provided him with an impenetrable carapace.

Barely standing on her feet, Lia narrowly dodged his sharp claws.

A few millimeters closer and her face would have been disfigured. the second paw came swooping towards her. She had just enough time to turn around but it was already too late.

She was thrown against a tree. Dazed, she could not get up. She groped the ground for her weapons. Frightened, she remembered that she had dropped them; now, she was weaponless and at the mercy of the beast.

The animal sniffed at her before grabbing her with its paw. Its claws penetrated her skin. Lia let out a scream. The animal squeezed harder. She was losing her breath when suddenly she collapsed to the ground. The animal, though alive, was not moving.

Just as she thought death was approaching, Kéo grabbed the fruit, mistaking it for a stone, and threw it to divert the beast's attention.

He rushed to Lia and helped her to sit down. She struggled to catch her breath.

"Are you OK? Are you hurt?" he said, panicking as much as humanly possible.

She looked at her body covered in scratch marks.

"It will pass. Let's get out of here," she said, pulling off her hemp belt to act as a bandage.

"Let's kill the beast first!" Kéo was looking for his weapon.

She then remembered Papilio's words.

"Maybe it wanted to protect itself?"

"From who? From us?" mocked Kéo.

"Let's go!" she said without replying to him.

Lia picked up her weapons and they followed the path the map indicated.

"But what was that fruit? I threw it thinking it would distract him, not knock him out?"

"A creature gave it to me. I'll tell you later. We're almost there."

"Another creature? This forest is more dangerous than I thought."

They finally arrived at the entrance of a cave.

"They are surely inside!" said Lia.

Kéo took the lead. As soon as they entered, they discovered several possibilities of passage, some of which went into the depths.

"Wait for me here, I'll make us a torch."

While waiting for him, Lia looked at the map, which did not mention any other path than the one to the cave. At the thought of entering the cave, she felt a chill that iced her to the spot. Kéo handed her a torch. They had no choice but to move forward.

"So what is the way?"

"It doesn't tell me that! Any ideas?"

Kéo examined the ground. He saw traces of something but they did not look like human steps.

"It's already a start," he said.

They went deeper into the darkness. The further they went, the more difficult it became to breathe.

They heard strange noises that sounded like whistling mixed with screaming.

Suddenly, the shadow cast by the torch distorted into two people, one of whom was killing the other. Lia closed her eyes and when she opened them again, her shadow was back to normal. She thought that fatigue was playing tricks on her.

A few moments later, her shadow did the same thing. Lia dropped the torch and cowered in terror in a dark corner. Her shadow enveloped her and forced visions upon her. She saw clearly the shadows of her father and herself. She killed him with several stab wounds, then the picture changed. Her sisters were lying on the ground, begging for her help and she turned away from them grinning. The scenes continued and each time Lia was cold and merciless. Lia sobbed in terror.

Relieved, the vision ended. Little by little, the shadow turned into a human with a white face and sharp teeth. He came to whisper to her.

"This is what your fate will be! You will turn into what you hate, because you will have failed, failed miserably. Your fear will lead you to become the shadow of yourself. Abandon all hope!"

Lia plugged her ears. She didn't want to hear him anymore. But he kept repeating the same words and grew louder and louder. She felt herself falling into an endless hole. She had the impression that her heart was failing her.

Then she came to in the cave, sweating and out of breath.

"What happened?" asked Kéo.

"What do you mean? You didn't feel anything?" she looked at him strangely.

"No, I was telling you that I saw human tracks when you passed out. I've never seen anyone like that before. Your eyes turned white, and you kept mumbling incomprehensible words."

"How did you wake me up?"

"I tried to wake you up, but it didn't work, so I did what I was taught in the past, I talked to your unconscious, trying to make you come to your senses. I mentioned your quest."

"Thank you!" she said with relief. "The atrocious visions were nothing but horror. It makes my blood run cold to think of reliving them."

"I don't know what's going on around here, but the cave must have caused exactly the same things to others."

Kéo helped her back on her feet. They continued on their way. At times something was trying to pull her back into the abyss, so she held on to what was most important to her—seeing her family again was the deepest thought she had. It was then that in a dark corner, they saw Emile and four other warriors.

They rushed towards them, and she grabbed Emile by the shoulders to try to wake him up. Nothing worked. Kéo was no more successful. Kéo was leaning over one of the men whom Lia recognized. She had met his eyes when she was in Iotopia. She immediately had an impression that she did not understand.

"As someone who has spent time with Emile, you must know some of his secrets. Try to talk to him, as I did for you," said Kéo, pushing her to try something.

She took Emile's face in her hands, and muttered.

"Hang in there, don't lose hope. You still have a lot to live for. Even, I am convinced, to start a family. So hold on to that, because one day you will wake up among the people you love and you will live the life that you have always wanted. You will live in peace, Emile."

Then Emile moved, and opened his eyes.

"You found me," his lips curled around his words "You didn't waste any time, I see. Did you miss me already?"

Then, he brought her head close to his and kissed her. Kéo cleared his throat.

"I don't want to disturb you both, but we have other people to wake up, and unless you know their deepest desires, I suggest you think of another way," said Kéo.

Emile stood up and helped Lia in turn.

"You're right, let's go hunt down that boogeyman!"

"The what?" asked Kéo.

"Boogeyman! Didn't your mother ever warn you about the boogeyman if you didn't behave?"

Kéo glared at him before adding.

"First the elves, then that strange bear and now what, a dream devourer?"

"What? You crossed the path of an owl bear and you are still alive. I underestimated you Kéo," Emile said smiling at him.

"What do you mean by underestimating?" Kéo squinted at him without a smile.

"Let's get back to the boogeyman, shall we?" said Lia.

"Indeed, a boogeyman steals dreams to replace them with nightmares. They feed on fears, and it allows them to be stronger."

"So he's not the only one?" asked a frightened Kéo.

"For now it is, but if we manage to kill it another one appears, nobody knows where they come from, nor their powers and how to stop them once and for all."

"How do we kill this one?" continued Kéo.

"It is important to know that he is not really human, he is a shadow. Swords, bows and other objects are useless. What you need to do is to find an object that belongs to him and destroy it. But be careful, when he feels really in danger, he uses nightmares to attack us, literally. The fire will push them back! Once destroyed, they will wake up."

"What do we do? Do we split up?" asked Kéo.

"Do you feel able to fight your nightmares?" mocked Emile.

"I could ask you the same question. It is not me, who fainted!" he replied staunchly.

"I think it's a bad idea. I managed to compel him once. I don't know if I'll be able to again," admitted Lia.

"Yes, let's stay together," agreed Kéo.

Emile relit his torch and started walking.

"He has the weapon we came for, and I suspect that his lair is in exactly the same place. We had started to follow a trail, it must have been this way, but it's a real labyrinth!"

They all remained silent, dreading the moment when one of their worst nightmares would arise. Everyone focused on happy memories. Lia thought of the times when her brothers and Eliad taught her how to fight and of their laughter.

Suddenly, she felt a chill wind, but nothing seemed to attack her. They took one of two paths at the next intersection, and the wind disappeared. That's when Lia remembered.

"Did you feel the cold wind as I did earlier?"

"Yes," both said.

"In some tunnels the wind is stronger, as if to push us to flee from it. Perhaps this is not the path we must take to reach his lair?"

"You're probably right," agreed Emile. "Let's go back."

They walked up the path to choose the one from which the wind came. That same icy wind hit them hard as they walked down the path.

The further they went, the more it blew. Suddenly dark thoughts came to her. Then she thought harder and looked at Kéo and Emile. Emile seemed to be suffering as much as she was, but Kéo remained the same. He seemed unperturbed.

Suddenly, something at the end of the corridor moved very fast, Kéo shouted.

" A shadow, get ready!"

A gigantic shadow in the shape of an owl-bear appeared. Emile rushed towards it and flooded it with his torch. It made a thud and disappeared.

"It's not over yet, so be on your guard. This means that we are not far away," shouted Emile.

An icy wind swirled around them and threatened to blow out their torches. Then a shadow approached. It was the same shadow that Lia had seen in her nightmare, the man with sharp teeth. He approached, muttering incomprehensible words. Emile and Lia were writhing in pain. Although they tried to think of positive things, the thing was stronger, and there was much darkness in its life.

She thought back to the day when everything changed, the attack, the separation from her family, the bloodshed and the war.

Then everything turned against her. It was all her fault, because they were after her to get something from her. He whispered something to her but, she was so far away that she didn't understand.

The closer she got, the more she began to hear what the shadow was telling her. She heard her name, then the name of King Solis, then the death of her father. Then he spoke of two girls, and just as he was about to say their names, Lia woke up next to Emile, who was as tormented as she was.

"What happened?" said Lia, breathing very fast.

"He was too strong. Where is Kéo? If we're still alive, the boogeyman must be dead."

"I am here!" approached Kéo sprinting. "I managed to get through the shadows, more than once. I thought my flashlight would go out. I managed to find the object and destroy it."

"Thank you Kéo," Lia and Emile answered in unison.

"Let's take what I came for and leave!"

Kéo and Lia followed Emile. The lair was full of objects, most of which were several years old.

"How did you recognize the object belonging to him?" asked Lia to Kéo.

"It was pretty obvious. It was the only one with a black color as if it was rotting itself."

"Ah here is the Gae Bolga!"

The four warriors joined them. Lia looked at the man with a captivating gaze. He looked at her, then asked Emile what had happened.

Lia took Kéo by the arm to question him.

"How come the thing didn't touch you?"

"Of course it did. It's just that I was thinking very hard about Rose. That must have been enough."

"No Kéo, before I fainted, I saw Emile suffering, and you nothing, not even a sign of weakness," she continued to ask fiercely.

He huffed as he looked at her, then put his hand on her shoulder before answering.

"As you know, I've come a long way. The less you know the better it is. I can only tell you that I have learned in times of war to shut off my mind so that no one can read my thoughts. My dad taught me to do this at a very young age, even though it is difficult."

"I know you don't like to talk about your past, but I hope one day you will."

Emile called to them from afar, and one of the four warriors handed them a canteen of water, which they gladly accepted.

"Let me introduce you to the Korrigans, here is the chief Amaric, then Daegan, Joao and Rohan."

Chief Amaric was the least handsome, and the smallest. He had long black hair, a hard face and a big mouth. Joao and Rohan were brothers; the first one had short blond hair and the second one had brown hair that was half-long but tied in a ponytail. Joao, the taller and thinner one, had a small scar on the corner of his mouth, on the right side. And although Lia saw red glints in his eyes under the torchlight, his eyes were blue. Rohan had small brown eyes, and a broad smile. She recognized Daegan, the one she had met in Iotopia, and who had given her that strange impression. He had laughing eyes, a square chin, but what Lia noticed were his two small dimples that deepened when he smiled.

Kéo brought her out of her thoughts when he spoke.

"It is urgent! Papilio sent us, a war is coming, they are going to be attacked by a powerful druid!"

"Arzel," replied Emile in a dry tone.

"Yes, he asked us to bring back the Gae Bolga weapon as soon as possible. Is this the one you are holding in your hand?"

He nodded his head in approval. The spear was made of bone and was covered with strange patterns.

Amaric addressed Emile.

"Tell King Solis that we will do this as soon as possible. We will gather our people. We will not leave them alone. If it is Arzel who is behind this, this war is not only theirs. Joan and Rohan will accompany you. Carrying this powerful weapon alone is far too dangerous. Let's leave now. It's best not to drag things out."

He greeted Lia and set off with Daegan on his way. They followed them to take the way back. Lia hoped they were not too late. They had lost a little more than a day with all these mishaps.

21

In battle

*L*ia was ready as soon as the assault was made. She was perched on a tree near the border of Iotopia. At her side stood the archers.

A scout came running, all out of breath. The enemy lines were coming.

When they returned, they had given the weapon to King Solis. He didn't show any sign of recognition and barely looked at Lia. She was angry, and her attitude did not bode well. Lia felt underestimated by the king, because he never said a kind word to her about what she had just done. She wondered if he would ever see her as anything other than a human. But she had not said her last word. She still had to survive this war.

Emile and Kéo were with the swordsmen. She hoped that the Koligans' help would arrive soon. This was her first war, and if she survived it, it would not be the last. She suddenly understood her father's harshness toward her. At that very moment when she was waiting to kill or be killed. It occurred to her how much the endurance of those years would help her overcome the terror of what was coming.

It was then that she saw a projectile thrown straight at one of the elves posted a few meters away from her. One of the elves shouted.

"Get ready!!! They are coming!"

Her heart began to pound, and then she saw one of the manticores. It was looking around as if it was waiting to kill. The manticores had a lion's body, a scorpion's tail, and a bat's wings. They had gigantic claws, and their head, although it looked like a lion, was bigger, which made them even more terrifying.

A few minutes later, a herd joined it and as if on cue, they attacked—the elves ordered to shoot. Lia managed to hit it target twice, but it wasn't enough to kill it. After three more arrows were fired, he finally fell to the ground.

The elves, on the other hand, knew their opponents and knew exactly where to shoot. A single arrow was enough to kill them. The fight was going to be difficult and Lia doubted more than anything else her ability to fight.

Seeing the elves fight gave her hope. She remembered Emile's words. They were indeed very good warriors. They were agile, they could step and jump as easily as children. They killed quickly enough. But no matter how hard they pushed them back, thousands more would come.

Suddenly, a group of dark elves appeared and two earth elves fell to the ground. Lia turned in time to dodge a blow.

There was nothing good about the dark elves anymore. Their yellow eyes were greedy, and their skin was parched and dirty. All of their elven features were amplified to give them an evil air. And They were much faster.

Lia was struggling to keep up when one of the elves came to her aid. They were now under attack from all sides. Lia managed to hit one of them. Now overwhelmed, they decided to attack them on the ground.

As Lia fought one of the dark elves, a manticore attacked her and rolled her a few feet away. She dodged its tail, but fighting a formidable animal of that size was difficult. With her sword, she managed to cut off the tip of its tail, and the beast screamed.

Just as it was about to pounce on her, her dog Spirit sprang up and jumped on it. He saved her life once again. She resumed the fight. She thought of Emile and hoped he was doing better than she was.

Although they had the advantage, the earth shifted, trembled, and opened under their feet and the trees attacked them. The druid Arzel was not far away. The fight became more difficult. Not only did they have to fight against monsters, but they also had to fight against the elements of nature.

Lia saw more than one elf die. In a moment of deep sadness, she did not see one of the dark elves raise his sword against her. One of the elves of King Solis' guard protected her by sacrificing his life.

Cordis helped her up.

"This is not the time to give up. Do you want to fight? Do you want to help your family? Then start here and now! If you can't stand up, then give up, because this fight is nothing compared to your destiny. It is time to take responsibility for what you are doing."

As he walked away, Lia measured his words and, with tears in her eyes, began to fight again with her dog at her heels. Those who had fallen should not have died for nothing.

She recognized Arzel at once. He was old, and wrinkled and wore long grey hair. He was wearing a long toga covered with bones and blood. He was holding a stick and moved forward quietly, looking down his nose at all the elves who were standing in front of him. All he had to do was wave his staff to disintegrate them. Lia and the elves were losing the battle.

One of the commanders asked them to retreat. They all retreated to the den, where they had built a huge wall of wood and brambles from the rose bushes. Once everyone had reached the lair, Lia understood the charm of these flowers. They held back, as if by magic, the evil spells of the druid who was striving to destroy all around him. But this did not stop the manticores or the dark elves. Some of them managed to climb on the makeshift wall.

Suddenly a hand was placed on Lia's shoulder. It was Emile.

"Are you OK? You're not hurt are you?" He glanced at Spirit. "I see that someone has found you!"

Lia allowed a faint smile to cross her face before spotting Joao and Rohan.

"I'm scared," she admitted.

"The opposite would be surprising. Sometimes fear is a good companion in war. It allows to survive."

Then, King Solis stood along the fence in a majestic way to challenge his enemies.

"It is too late Arzel, you may destroy us but our knowledge will never belong to you," he said loudly and strongly.

"You think I came for your powers? They are nothing compared to Aergad," laughed Arzel.

"It's impossible. He is dead!" the king said sharply.

"If you believe it," by taking an evil air. "My last words will be Mélana and Néa have been found!"

For the first time, Lia saw King Solis' face contort in anguish. He raised his hands to the sky and whispered words in a language she did not understand. A flock of birds came to attack the manticores.

An earth elf commanded all the archers to attack, and they sent as many arrows as possible at the beasts. They managed to kill some of them but it was not enough to slow them down.

The manticores and dark elves had managed to penetrate the defenses. Lia had lost sight of Arzel. With Emile at her side, they fought back to back, protecting each other.

Cries of despair reached the earth elves. The roses turned black and disintegrated at once. The barrier exploded and threw everyone around it, including King Solis. Lia threw herself to protect him, and Emile, Cordis, Joao, Rohan and other elves joined her. Helping her as best they could to get up and walk, Lia lost her balance. She could not avoid the arrow that lodged itself in her right shoulder. Emile ran over.

"How are you?" he leaned towards her.

"I can still stand!" she was trying her best to stand up straight.

Although wounded, Lia pushed Emile away from her, avoiding an assault. They were overwhelmed by numbers.

As they tried to fend them off, Arzel slowly approached, savoring his victory.

Just as Lia thought all hope was lost, spears and pilums flew at their enemies. The Korrigans had come.

Lia saw a man of imposing stature, short, with a long red beard approaching alongside Armaric and Daegan. They smiled at her. The man approached King Solis and forced a substance down his throat.

The effect was immediate, without a word, King Solis stood up and attacked. Everyone regained hope, ran toward their enemies, and fought with strength.

King Solis brandished the Gae Bolga and attacked the disintegrating enemies. Arzel saw this and raised his rowan and cast his spell on King Solis. But nothing happened, the spear countered all magical attacks. That's why it was so important!

As he fought, Arzel struggled to keep up. He retreated, fell back, lost his balance and fell to the ground. He dodged a blow from King Solis, got up and fled. King Solis raised the Gae Bolga and threw it in his direction. The spear whistled and flew around the trees before hitting him head-on. A cloud of dust formed around him.

Arzel had disappeared with the spear. The moment he disappeared, the dark elves and the manticores fled before the eyes of the elves and the Korrigans who began to shout their victory.

Lia ran into Emile's arms relieved that this battle was finally over.

A few hours later, the women joined the victorious fighters. Kéo found Rose, who must have been mortified. As for Lia, she joined Emile and the Korrigans around the fire. Emile gave her a drink. He talked about what he was going to do next. He said he would be leaving soon for Martyrs's Mountain to retrieve their artillery before going to help their allies, the Animas. Emile spoke with Armaric.

"Emile, are you leaving again? I thought you were coming with me?" asked Lia worried.

He took her in his arms and they walked together under Daegan's eyes.

"Lia, although your war is important, what I didn't tell you is that it was the Korrigans who took me in as a child. Although I never saw my adoptive parents again, I feel close to them. They have their own war, and I have to help them. I hope you understand. Orion is not dead. No one saw him on the battlefield. We all think that he must have tricked Arzel and that he is preparing a war against us and the Animas. Moreover, Arzel although wounded, remains an enemy to be found!"

"The Animas? What war?"

"Stakes are rising. The Animas are the closest allies of the Korrigans. They are great warriors but have few resources. It is my duty to help them."

"I thought you would come with me. I don't know what to do anymore, King Solis is not ready to help me and I don't know where to turn," Lia saddened.

"Maybe you should come with us? If you can't find help here, maybe you can find it with the Korrigans. But before you rush off, talk to King Solis one last time. I saw him heading to the shrine. He was alone, now is the time."

He hugged her for a moment, but Lia remained pensive before regaining courage. She hurried back to the sanctuary where King Solis was sitting with Papillo, murmuring.

"It's time to tell me the truth," she was screaming. "I'm not a child anymore. Now it's time to know if you're going to help me or not. what's the point of making me stay here? How do you know my mother?"

Papillo understood and went out to let them talk. King Solis pointed to a seat where she sat down before speaking.

"Man has the fascinating ability to forget. He is so down to earth. Anything that seems out of time, and inexplicable is considered impossible and then becomes, as he calls it, a myth, a legend. When asked where this legend comes from, they answer; *from the imagination of a madman.* Man has never been willing to accept the impossible, let alone be helped. I'm sorry, man has been weak for a long time, and I can't do anything about it. I cannot fight for a cause that is already long lost, at the risk of destroying all that I have achieved so far. I cannot forget the suffering of women and children caused by the cruelty of men. Men who were deemed too weak, destroyed and humiliated for having been so. Your mother was broken forever. How do I forgive man?"

"I don't agree. Certainly we have faults, but also qualities, such as that of loving. I grant you, and I have witnessed it, man can be cruel without limits and sometimes excels in this field thanks to his imagination. But there are good people in this world, willing to fight to stay good, willing to fight to survive. There are also people who have given their lives for strangers, in the name of hope. I will never stop fighting as long as that glow persists. It has never been extinguished in all these years, only weakened. But today I see it bigger than ever. Maybe we will fail but I will have done it without any regrets because I will have fought for people who are afraid and waiting to be saved. Waiting and hoping is so much easier than fighting! I forgive them. And do you know why? Because I have enough strength for them. I will never give up. Sometimes I may want to give up but I remember all the good in this world, in every beating heart. We just have to destroy the rest. I have enough love to heal the world. If I give up, it will kill me. I will do it with or without your help."

"It's honorable, but you weren't there when it all started. The war that man initiated, destroyed all that was good on this earth. We just escaped the slaughter," he said darkly.

"If you won't do it for me, then do it for my mother. Caroline needs to be saved," panted Lia.

"Caroline?" he asked with surprise.

"Yes, my mother. You did tell me that you know her, didn't you?" asked Lia.

"No, her sister, Caroline, I never knew. I see…"

She looked at him, intrigued. He took the time to think, to choose his words before continuing.

"I can see why she preferred to keep it a secret. Maybe after this, you'll change your mind. Your mother's name is Maria. Caroline is her sister, which makes her your aunt."

"What? I don't believe you! Why are you hiding all this from me? I don't understand. how do you know that?" she said with a voice full of grief.

"I loved your mother. The man who later became a druid killed her and everything he could. Your sisters too."

"Sister?" she was trying to put all together. "How is this possible? I spent my childhood in the Colombier! You are lying!"

"I'm afraid not. Your aunt must have found a way to keep you as a baby when she picked you up to save you. I'm sorry to hear that. She shouldn't have kept the truth from you."

Lia did not understand anything anymore. She had been lied about her origins, her family wasn't really family even though they had heart ties. Everything she had built was based on a lie.

Everything was becoming clear now. She had always felt different. She was unlike any member of her family. Her grandparents hated her. Now she understood. What she felt now was confusion and resentment. All she felt was anger toward her family. They had no right to hide from her who she really was, it was her history, her past.

"Where is my father?" she said almost in tears.

"I don't know. We had a long relationship with your mother, but she never talked about her life and I only knew what she wanted to show me about herself. She was very discreet, but she had your smile and your kindness. The only thing I know for sure is that your mother would have wanted you to be safe here with us. Stay Lia. You belong here!"

"No, I don't belong anywhere. I don't know who to believe anymore. I ... I need time..." she said, with a tear slipping down her cheek.

She left the room upset. She needed advice from her friends. Maybe it was time to make other decisions. This betrayal was unbearable for her. She needed to come to her senses. Perhaps she should continue her quest or try to understand?

Emile saw her, but she waved him off. She entered the hut so hastily that she did not bother to close the door behind her.

"Kéo, Rose," she screamed, with tears in her eyes. "Where are you?"

She went back to their room, and found their bag on their back. A scribbled paper lay on the bed. They looked embarrassed as she picked up the letter. The first words overwhelmed her right away.

They had given up on her, they had lost all hope in her cause, and they no longer wanted to be involved in the danger she was causing. She turned to them in tears, her voice trembling.

"Are you leaving?" she was shivering with sadness.

He tried avoided her eyes, "It's complicated Lia."

"Complicated?" she yelled. "You were going to leave without a word."

"The letter was there to explain to you," said Rose

"You've lost hope, and you're leaving me alone, right?"

"Listen Lia," Rose took her hands. "We have to think about our future too."

She walked away from them, broken and disappointed.

"Then you leave, I am alone, what you represented in my eyes was only lies!" she was boiling inside, with tears in her eyes. "I was sincere in our friendship. Being able to sacrifice myself for it. As for you … you don't even grant me the honesty. Is friendship of no value to you? Is reaching out to me so unimportant? To leave like this… I don't recognize you," she said, falling apart.

Kéo approached her. "Lia…"

"No, go away!"

"Please…"

"GO!" she squealed, covering her eyes with her palms.

She sat for a moment. She was heartbroken. She had believed in their sincere friendship. She felt crushed by all these revelations. Bitterly disappointed, she didn't want to hear much more. Are we always alone in life? Can we not trust anyone?

She felt helpless again, but now she knew what decision she needed to make.

Lia dried her tears and took her bag to join Emile and the Korrigans.

"I am ready to go with you," she said stiffly.

"Lia, are you sure? It's the pain that makes you talk like that, I don't want you to regret it one day," said Emile concerned.

"I'm sure," said Lia looking sure and hurt.

As they began to leave, King Solis called out to him.

"If I'm not mistaken, you are running away, Lia!" he said in a last chance to stop her.

"You are mistaken, and I am not running away. I don't know who I am anymore. I was surrounded by cowards and hypocrites. That's the only truth. And you are one of them. I don't want to stay with you or with the one I used to call my family," she turned her back to him and took the step accompanied by Spirit under the sorry glance of her companions.

She never wanted to hear from her family again. She was devastated. She felt so far from home, so far from her life. She couldn't project herself and regain hope. She felt more alone than ever. She was cold, she was sad and she had lost everything. Tears were streaming down her face, she could feel them surging like a dagger. There was no respite for her mind as she kept thinking about the past and the future, which was looking more than chaotic. She had lost her faith and her identity.

She was moving forward, determined to put her past behind her and start a new life.

22

The hell

*A*yana felt empty, as if her whole being had no strength to exist. She didn't feel anything anymore, neither happiness, nor love, nor even hate … nothing.

She felt so lost in this black hole, without finding who she was. Hunger, breathing, waking up, all those things that make us human, were gone. Nothing could compare to this pain, to this despair that was eating her up from the inside. Just breathing became unbearable for her. She had to hide her feelings, she had to stay strong, despite this dark situation.

Ayana and Monica had been transported in a cage for over a month. They were cold and hungry. They were exhausted and scared. What had happened at the Colombier, they were paying for it today, it was the price of this chaos.

Although this war made no sense to them, the path they were taking was the most obscure. They were afraid to die, afraid that the last image they would keep of their parents, of their family, would be linked to this bloodbath. Not understanding the reasons for this was all the more painful for them.

Monica said that all their family members were dead, but Ayana didn't want to hear it. If she started to assume that, what little hope she had would not be enough to give her the courage to survive what was about to happen to them.

Now Ayana was just trying to sleep and avoid thinking about it all, despite the sobs of her sister, Monica. They were not alone. They had kidnapped other women and men and children as well.

The terror on their faces seemed more insurmountable than their own. Their father had taught them to rise above any situation, even if at this moment, the worst was more frightening than she could imagine.

Ayana stayed in her sister's arms, and tried to find sleep. But neither of them could. The anxiety kept them awake and the men who were watching them kept pestering them with garbage to prevent them from falling asleep. This amused them a lot. Some men were even more libidinous than the others. They would go after the older women. At each stop, they would take them into the forest to rape them. Ayana feared that they were destined for darker fates.

She then remembered Tharsile trying to help them and wounded, collapsing to the ground, while she tried to comfort Monica. They could only hope that he was still alive. It was perhaps their last hope.

The cart stopped, and the men paused again. Once again, one of them approached and opened the door.

"You!"

He pointed to a half-asleep older woman. When she realized she was the target, she started to scream and beg.

"Please! Not yet, please!"

Ayana plugged her ears. She couldn't stand to hear the screaming and crying anymore. Her sister took her hand and smiled.

Sometimes to pass the time, she would tell her stories or talk about her childhood. Ayana let her sister think that this was helping her, but it was not. She was too sad and terrified to be happy.

The ordeal of this poor woman had lasted for hours. Although they were all facing the same fate, they did not speak to each other. Ayana didn't know if it was out of fear or just because each of them had too much pain to comfort the others.

The man emerged from the forest, but this time alone. He approached the cage and said to the other men.

"Hey! Bad news, the old lady is dead!"

"Too bad, it will make less entertainment."

They all began to laugh, while some of them began to cry. In the cart, the fear was palpable, the anxiety of being next. She could feel it because she felt exactly the same way.

The men who were carried in another cart were lifeless. They had given up all desire to fight.

They set off again. It took a few hours to reach a village. It was commonplace, although she didn't see any women, as if men reigned supreme.

There were people everywhere, people shouting to sell their goods. You could find everything from scarves to silk dresses, food, weapons... There were so many things that one lost one's mind. The village was like a business fair of all kinds.

They arrived at what looked like the main square. In the middle stood a dais with a post to condemn people to, benches set up around it. As for the mansion that overlooked the square, it was large and decorated with a balcony the width of the building.

The guards led the women out, while hundreds of men booed them and reached out to try to grope them. The guards protected them, although they let those who offered them a ticket a feel. They pushed the women into a corridor and locked them in a cell.

As for the men and children, they were taken to another building.

The cell was small and smelled of blood and vomit. Other girls were already crowding in. They were crowded together because the cell held more people than it could hold.

They had been imprisoned for two days now. They had not received any visits or food. Nothing. The other women told of the torments that had been done to them. To survive, they advised to accept whatever they wanted to do.

Ayana thought that she couldn't be more afraid than she is now, but she was wrong... The story of these women didn't help to reassure her. Their fate was getting darker by the minute.

***

On the third day, a guard came and took one of the girls, who was in the cart with Ayana and Monica. She was gone for hours, until it was Ayana's turn.

Her heart was beating fast as she was led through a long corridor that distributed cells just as morbid as theirs. Screams came from every corner, some calling for help, others rambling or asking to die. She heard moans and groans and realized that men were being tortured. She walked through pools of blood from the dungeons.

She imagined her worst fears. What was going to happen to her?

They entered a large room, although it was sparsely furnished for such a large space. There was no window, just a few tables with bracelets to tie people to, and then all sorts of instruments that were probably used for torture. In the center was a chair, two armrests and handcuffs.

At the back of the room, an imposing throne overlooked the room with a small man sitting on it. Rather thin with thick hair that probably reached to the small of his back, but which he wore in a ponytail.

He wasn't the shortest man she had ever met, but he wasn't very tall. On the other hand, she had never seen anyone so strong, although her brothers were strong enough. He was pretty seasoned. His arms must have been his most muscular part.

She lost hope of surviving the meeting at the mere thought of her brothers. His face was not really ugly, but his posture and his haughty look took away all his charm. She was made to sit in the middle chair. She was so scared that she felt as if no words would ever come out of her mouth again.

A tray full of food was placed a few steps away. The man on his throne first smiled, although it looked more like a grimace, then asked the guards to step back and he spoke.

"Name me Balthazar. Yes, Balthazar runs this village with a firm hand. But before he begins any negotiations, he'll tell you where we are and what your life will be like."

He gave one of his monstrous smiles. She had the impression that he liked to hear himself talk, expressing himself in the third person, he seemed to love only himself. Ayana felt she had to be careful not to say the wrong word.

"Well, this village gloriously called *Servus* is a place of bargaining. You can find everything, EVERYTHING," he said, dripping with precision and pride. "Even girls. Balthazar says it modestly, our girls are very famous here. Most of the buyers, although less important than me, are in their province. There are also cruel people, but if you answer well, Balthazar can help you find a better home. You see, he can refuse a sale. He's the king, the god of this town, you see? Oh, yes! Balthazar remembers a girl. Although he can't remember her name, he remembers that she was very beautiful but stubborn. Unfortunately, she didn't cooperate. Balthazar had to send her to a terrible place, simply because she didn't tell the truth. The truth is so important, don't you think? She had to hold out for maybe a week at the whims of this man, whom Balthazar must recognize as being very twisted. But what do you expect, when he makes promises, he keeps them. And business is business. I hope you'll be cooperative. Balthazar never likes to send one of his daughters to a bad fate. Well, let's get started, shall we? If you answer, the food will be yours—just one question. What's your name?" he said playfully.

"Ayana," she said cautiously.

"Well, that's easy to answer, isn't it? Well, well, where are you from?"

"From the village of Colombier."

"Well, how old are you?"

"Twenty years."

"Nice age if you want his opinion. Thanks to me, Balthazar, maybe love will come. Maybe the man who buys you will be a kind of Prince Charming, who knows? Let's continue, shall we? Do you have any brothers or sisters? And where are your parents?"

"My sister Monica is with me. As for my parents, they died during the assault. '

'Oh, *my dear*, what a relief. Believe me, Balthazar, parents are just a burden. That's why he will never have a child. He won't become one of those matrons. Well, do you know any of these people living in the Colombier? What was your occupation?'

"I worked at the tavern. Although I once saw one of the sons of the village chief, I never had the opportunity to talk to any of them."

"You look very wise. That's very good for you, because you see the men over there," he pointed to three men who were supposed to have returned during his interview, "they would have served as punishment, but thanks to your honesty, you just saved them a lot of trouble. Although Balthazar is not afraid to hit a woman, you must remain perfect, and intact for the day of your sale. For now, Balthazar doesn't need you. He's trying to get to know each of you. But we'll meet again later, Ayana."

He smiled at her again. This time it gave her a shiver.

When she returned to her cell, she did not see Monica. She, too, had been taken away for questioning. Ayana was worried. By lying, she thought she was doing right by her family. Their secrets had to be kept. In any case, not being part of the male gender of the house, she knew very little about the mysteries that hung over her family. But then, she hadn't thought that Monica could tell the truth. She was so fragile.

The hours were passing and this did not bode well. That's when Monica entered the cell. She had cried so much that her face was deformed. Monica was not even given time to hug her sister. A guard violently grabbed Ayana, who barely had time to hear her sister's words.

"I'm sorry!"

This time, the guards did not go in the same direction. Ayana immediately realized that Balthazar had discovered her lie. She thought they were going to play with her before killing her.

During the whole walk, she implored for mercy. If there was a powerful being, she asked him to forgive her and to let her die faster in order to free herself from all these afflictions that had destroyed what she was.

She let herself be pushed, then carried by the guards who ended up dragging her to the ground. They crossed the courtyard. She thought they were taking her to the post, but to her astonishment, they went around it and into the big house.

The little man was sitting in front of the fireplace drinking what looked like coffee. Seeing her so frightened, he said to her.

"Take a seat, don't look so shy! Balthazar is giving you a second chance to tell him the truth. You see, you've got potential, and you and your sister could make me a lot of money. But as he's already told you, the truth is all that matters to him. Balthazar holds a grudge, a very big grudge. Be careful not to make him

285

angry. As much as he loves money, there's always a limit to what he can do. Don't you think?"

He handed her a cup of coffee, which she refused.

"Don't refuse, little one, this gesture of kindness. He does not advise you to do so!"

She took the coffee cup trembling. She waited for him to address her. He sang as if he had forgotten her presence. Then he turned away his cruel little eyes and smiled at her.

"Well will you? Let's get started! You just have to answer the questions, nothing easier."

"If you know who I am, I don't have to answer questions. Send me back to my cell."

"Silly or brave? Although courage, Balthazar finds it STUPID!" he was turning red with rage.

He spilled the cup of coffee in her hands and waved to the guards posted behind her. They went into the next room, and returned with a man and a woman. They tied the man to a chair. Balthazar stood up and beat him.

"My dear, you don't leave Balthazar much choice. He has to react accordingly. It hurts him that you are not cooperating."

"Wait, I'm sorry, let me try again."

She didn't want to see anyone being bullied, or hurt by her.

"Too late, my dear, too late. If you were like Balthazar, you would know what it takes to stay a leader."

She watched helplessly as the man was tortured. Several times they forced her to watch, threatening to attack the woman if she did not comply. Unable to bear this scene, Ayana lost consciousness.

An unbearable smell woke her up. She didn't know how long she had been unconscious. This nauseating smell emanated from the water he had thrown in her face.

"You left us no choice. Urine is a great way to wake up a sleeping bear," he laughed out loud before resuming. "Don't worry *dear*, we don't send our girls to the sale without a bath. You missed the best one. It's a pity, he's dead! Ah ah ah … he didn't last very long. It's half the fun."

Then he signaled the guards to bring the woman, and let go of them.

"Have fun boys!"

Horrified, Ayana rushed her confession and shouted.

"My name is Ayana. That's my real name. My father was George Leusire and my mother Caroline Leusire. I have four brothers and three sisters. My father ran the Colombier. But I know nothing more. I don't know anything about my father's secrets."

Out of exhaustion and disappointment, she fell to her knees and immediately began to cry. Balthazar motioned for the woman to be returned to her cell. Although she had spared her a dark fate, her future did not look any better.

"Well, I told you the truth always pays off. Confessing that you are from an important lineage will change your fate. You and your sister will be sent to a powerful leader, not the worst or the best. You won't even have to go through the auction. You're lucky. Even if Balthazar didn't like your behavior, he's giving you a chance, because you'll bring him a lot of money, you and your sister, a lot. In the meantime, for the next two weeks, try to sleep and enjoy the festivities of the auctions. It's lovely and so distracting!"

He jumped up and down in excitement. They led Ayana to her cell where Monica was waiting impatiently. She embraced her and begged her forgiveness.

"I don't blame you, Monica. This place is cursed. We're just trying to survive in our own way. The important thing is that we stay together."

23

Everything is getting darker

Ayana and Monica were standing on the balcony behind Balthazar. As for the other girls, they were all lined up behind the post.

It was crowded, most of the important people who had come to attend the sale had sat on the benches. Many people had come from far and wide. There was food, music and even dancers who performed an exotic ballet to entice the customers.

Ayana and Monica did not know any of the girls. Those who had made the trip with them would be sold in two weeks, the day that they will be leaving.

They did not understand why they were attending this event. They were nothing more than unimportant commodities. Balthazar beckoned them forward.

"Girls, have fun! It's a day of celebration," he clapped his hands, "let's bring champagne to these ladies."

Ayana and Monica looked at each other puzzled. They took a drink, although they were not in the mood for a party. They couldn't refuse a drink. They were so afraid to make him angry. The images of their last meeting with him will always be engraved in their memory.

"Balthazar must admit that he is not used to such generosity, but your benefactor made me a large offer to entertain you. What generosity, Balthazar was most touched. Because he likes you, he will give you a tip. Such generosity often hides dark things. Beware, above all do not grieve him. Serious things happen when one disobeys. Dear Ayana, you have seen this. If you want to be happy, make him happy! If Balthazar is giving you this advice, it's because he hopes you won't disappoint him. He doesn't want to lose this very good customer. Girls come and go. You are only of real value if the man has his eye on you, so Balthazar's interest becomes quite different. Losing a girl is not so sad. Balthazar just loses a way to get more money. So don't get your hopes up about my possible fascination with you, because it's not. Enjoy the festivities!"

He motioned for them to get back in their seats. They hardly looked at what was happening, and it saddened them to see these women sold like cattle.

Some of them were acting like animals, excited about their find so they could fulfill their worst desires.

Ayana no longer even hoped to fall into a good home. The power here had such a bad taste. She couldn't imagine an honest man coming to buy a girl. The festivities continued, and the women followed one another. One after the other, they climbed onto the stage. The most beautiful ones didn't need to wiggle to attract attention, but the less attractive ones had to strip off their clothes as they went along.

Suddenly, one of them, now half-naked, had failed to seduce a buyer among the assembly of men.

Balthazar nodded to one of the guards standing next to her. He grabbed her and pulled her violently toward the crowd of obviously less wealthy men. They raised bills to the guard, who gladly accepted them and sent the woman into the crowd, which dragged her inside.

Ayana and Monica looked at the scene, horrified. The women who had not made a profit had been handed over to gangs of thugs.

Ayana had never imagined such atrocities. She had never considered the world so cruel. She understood her father more than ever, all his messages, the hard and demanding education he had given to his children. He understood that sometimes the world has a brutal way of making us feel so miserable.

There were still girls left, and it was torturous to watch. Ayana wished that she would never again see a single woman thrown to these beasts.

Suddenly, her sister elbowed her in the ribs to attract her attention. A guard had just entered the balcony, he was wearing exactly the same outfit as the guards of that kingdom, black boots and pants, blue shirt, and a big red belt. Ayana had a lapse of time before recognizing him in this accouterment.

"But, it's Tharsile!" she whispered to her sister.

He had managed to infiltrate, so all hope was not lost. However, Ayana found it difficult to see a way out. Even if they managed to get out of the prison, it seemed impossible to leave the village. They could be attacked at any moment by the men of the village who had no humanity left.

But she left these unanswered questions aside in order to enjoy the joy of his coming.

An hour later, the guards were taking them back to their cells. They passed in front of Tharsile, who pretended not to see them.

Just before the last corridor that led them to their dungeon, Tharsile appeared and whispered something in the guards' ears. The next moment, the guards left the corridor, leaving them alone with him.

Tharsile hugged Monica for a few seconds.

"I have to be quick before the guards come back. We don't have much time. I am part of the guard of the man who bought you. The only way out is to get to his house. Don't worry. You're not alone anymore."

"Our parents, our family?" asked Ayana.

He lowered his voice.

"I don't know if they are still alive, I'm sorry. Please pretend you don't know me. I'm sorry I can't help you now."

"You're here, that's the main thing," said Monica, taking his hand.

With these last words, they returned to the cell. Ayana had never seen Monica so peaceful since their capture. And she understood her. If she, too, saw the man she loved still alive, she couldn't be happier.

***

The two weeks went by fairly quickly, although they sometimes heard people screaming and women coming back in shock.

They had not seen Balthazar again, who was preoccupied with the organization of the festivities that were to welcome the highest ranks of society.

The girls were selected with great care. They brought them out of the dungeon with the girls chosen for the occasion. They were the last in line. The girls took the path that led to the courtyard, while they went to the balcony. The deal was done. Already promised to their buyer, they were not to be mixed up in the sale of the day.

When they reached the balcony, Monica gripped Ayana's hand tightly, her face horrified. She bent down and saw Tharsile tied to the post, and swollen. Balthazar stared at them. For a moment, they imagined that he had understood that they knew him and discovered his identity.

"Oh, girls, don't look so downcast, have you ever seen a man about to die. Stop your childishness!"

Ayana whispered in Monica's ear.

"He has to have an explanation, don't cry. We could make things worse if he finds out the truth. I know, it's hard, but I'm here. Think of something else. Think of father and mother. Please be strong."

Her words sounded false. She didn't know how to reassure her. If she were in his place she would be just as devastated.

Suddenly a sturdy man in his forties, tall, with beautiful blue eyes, short blond hair, dressed in elegant gold embroidered clothes, and wearing a red hat, smiled at them before turning to Balthazar.

"Balthazar, would you release this man?"

"Oh Armand, good to see you. But this man tried to steal food and you know how Balthazar doesn't like lies and thieves."

"Of course, but this man is of great importance to me, as are your daughters. What if offer you financial compensation?"

"That would be most interesting indeed, but what about Balthazar's reputation? Imagine if it were known that he had made a gesture of grace. What would my credit be? I'm sorry, but I'm afraid I'll have to decline."

"Know that I have thought about this of course," he gave a signal to his guards to bring the handcuffed man. "Here is the man you will kill, say that he confessed to be the thief."

"Um ... in that case, it's a deal. How much are you offering me for the damages?" looking at the purse filled with coins.

"The amount of your choice," he looked at Ayana and Monica, "are they my girls?"

"Yes, is something wrong?"

"No, on the contrary, they are more beautiful than they were described to me. Let them be ready in an hour. I must hurry. I'm afraid I have family business to attend to. I beg your pardon. I want you to know that with me, your reputation will take a completely different path. I guarantee you your fortune."

"Oh, thanks to you, sir. May your trip be the sweetest. Come back whenever you want. You will be my guest forever."

"Thank you!" he said, shaking the purse with a big smile.

He got up and stomped off while Balthazar asked for Tharsile to be replaced. Monica smiled, Ayana understood, although she was sorry for the man's fate, no one had the right to condemn a life.

During the last hour in that cursed village, they watched in relief as Tharsile was freed, and then the death of that other man at the stake. As he screamed, the sales continued, some finding death entertaining. As one of the women wiggled on the platform, Tharsile came to fetch them.

"Oh my dears, good luck in your new home. As for you, young man, thank your master once again.

How hectic life is!" Balthazar sat back down as they left with a more confident step.

Tharsile made them get into a carriage. Their buyer Armand was not there, so Ayana asked Tharsile.

"Where is Armand?"

"He never travels in the presence of a woman. The journey is long. It takes a day."

"I'm so relieved you didn't get burned," then she hugged him.

"I feel guilty for this man. I was trying to steal food for you and the other women."

"You wanted to do well," Ayana looked at him worried, which he guessed.

"What are you thinking about? Speak up! Don't be afraid!"

"Can you tell me what happened at the Colombier?"

Monica detached herself from him and waited for him to answer.

"Well, I'll try but I don't have all the answers. As soon as I saw you trapped, I ran to try to rescue you."

He recounted the struggle of their brothers, the disappearance of their sisters and their mother, and the last image of his brothers and his father imprisoned.

"I managed to pass myself off as someone close to King Theodore. Being a royal guard, it is easy for me to know things that few people know. He thinks he can get closer to King Hilarion by taking me under his wing."

When he finished, no one spoke a word. Ayana took advantage of this moment to sleep.

During the whole trip, she had nightmares. Monica woke her up to tell her that they had just arrived. When she got out of the carriage, Ayana saw the house, which was not very big but beautiful.

It was a sublime mansion. The door was on the left side with a beautiful flowerbed. In the middle there was a small waterfall, its raised center that could be reached by a small path, contained flowers of all varieties. There was a stable and pens for the horses. The whole courtyard was covered with a multitude of flowers, including many roses.

They were not directed to the main door, but to a smaller one on the opposite side.

A maid was waiting for them on the doorstep. She was old, her hair was greasy and unkempt, and she was tall but fat and wrinkled. She looked them up and down and looked hostile.

"Tharsile, thank you, I'll take it from here."

"Well," he gave them a last look before getting back into the coach.

"Welcome to Purism! Please come in, ladies."

They entered the kitchen. There was a table on the side, a fireplace on the opposite side and two armchairs on the front. In the back of the room were ovens and, in the extension, the kitchen counter.

"My name is Berthe. I will be your housekeeper. Your duties in this house are, for the time being, to wash the kitchen and other rooms that I will show you, and then to cook. If you don't know how to cook, you will be taught. A few rules; never speak in the presence of men, nor in the presence of anyone more important than yourself and myself. Wait until you are given the floor to speak. Never go beyond this room and the one I am about to show you. If any of these rules are broken, then a severe punishment will be allocated. I forgot, never refuse a task you are asked to do. Never, is that clear?" she said sharply.

They nodded, then without giving them time to say a word, she led them to the third door near the entrance.

This door led to a small L-shaped corridor, then at the end, a door leading to the outside to hang the laundry, then another one, that of the cabinet, and in the opposite corner, a lot of wood. There was a staircase that was forbidden to use, a vestibule to put jackets and coats, and next to it a narrow room with two small beds, cupboards and a shelf.

"This will be your room! Tomorrow, first thing in the morning, I'll introduce you to Gisele who will teach you how to cook" with these words, she slammed the door without showing a sign of kindness.

They were obviously not welcome, but although the welcome was not the warmest, Ayana felt good. She didn't sense any hostility. She didn't know how long she would be here, but she thought she would like her new life.

In the morning, they were awakened by a noise inside the room. A skinny young woman was patting the bed.

"Sorry, I didn't know how to wake you up. But you're late. You'll have to find a way to stop being late. Luckily for you, Berthe left very early for the market, otherwise you would have been in serious trouble. Get dressed quickly and meet me in the kitchen."

"Wait! Are you Gisele?" asks Monica.

"Yes," she left with a final smile.

Dressed, they arrived in the kitchen where the pleasant scent of warm bread was spreading.

"If one of you can keep turning what I'm cooking, while the other helps me prepare the dough.

While helping her, Ayana took the opportunity to gather some information.

"This house is beautiful!"

"Yes, it can be", answering her in a nonchalant tone.

"This looks like a nice place to live" continued Monica.

Gisele turned around to make sure no one could hear her.

"It may look like it, but in reality it is full of slander."

"What do you mean?" asked Ayana intrigued.

"I shouldn't be telling you this, but considering your rank, I'll take the liberty of telling you. Promise you'll keep it a secret."

"Of course," said Ayana.

"Last week, a girl died because she refused to sleep with a man. They beat her to death. As for me," she showed us her back full of scars, "I got the ingredients for the pie wrong. Mistakes are serious here, but if it makes you feel better, as long as we don't sleep on the floor, we are not asked to do anything inappropriate."

"How long have you been here?" asked Monica.

"Five years. As long as things are done right, there's no reason to be afraid!"

Paradise had suddenly turned into hell. They had to find a way out at all costs. They would not survive here for long. Ayana hoped that Tharsile already had a plan.

"All my thoughts are lost
in my head, the more I think about it,
the more it is black."

Monica

About the author

Giulia Elohi

For years, I have walked this earth in search of a light, my light. As I embarked on one of my greatest adventures in the United States, I opened the door to incredible worlds of enchantment. Life always begins with a little magic.

https://giuliaelohi.com